Poor Unfortunate Soul

A Tale of the Sea Witch

By Serena Valentino

Autumn
Publishing

Autumn
Publishing

Published in 2018
by Autumn Publishing
Cottage Farm
Sywell
NN6 0BJ
www.igloobooks.com

Written by Serena Valentino
Adapted in part from Disney's *The Little Mermaid*

GRA005 0418
4 6 8 10 9 7 5
ISBN 978-1-78810-769-3

Printed and manufactured in Italy

*Dedicated to my mom and pops
for all their love and support*

*And to the memory of my bewitching feline
writing companion, Pflanze, who I miss dearly
—Serena Valentino*

PROLOGUE

A dark grey mist followed Ursula like creeping tentacles as she made her way through the seemingly abandoned town of Ipswich. Ursula's laugh echoed through the boarded-up cottages, their pitiful denizens huddled within, terrified of the vengeful sea goddess who had descended upon them like a waking nightmare.

She had altered herself into her human form for the excursion, and used her magic to control the mists, creating long menacing tentacles for herself that curled around and trailed behind her, blighting everything they touched. She left a path of destruction in her wake, black like oil and putrefying.

She moved towards the main square and stood beneath the clock tower. Her tentacles assaulted it, turning the pillar into a wide black obelisk that might have been used for more sinister purposes than keeping time.

Hate.

Her magic was infused with it. And in that hate was a deep, penetrating sorrow. Those humans had taken from her the only person who had loved her, and she was going to make them suffer. She cast her ghostly appendages towards the sea, calling forth her dark minions.

Sirens.

These were a hideous mix of human and sea creature, like something conjured by the most deranged, visionary mind. Pale, haunting beings with dark smouldering pits for eyes emerged from the sea. Wide grinning mouths gnashed endless rows of sharp yellow teeth. Their skin was like thin, translucent milk, and through it one could see their deep blue veins and grotesque endoskeletons.

Though their song caused humans to tremble

and their ears to bleed, it was beautiful to Ursula. She found it winsome, intoxicating and overwhelmingly beautiful. Its haunting melody compelled those vile humans to emerge from their boarded dwellings, drawn to the siren song and spellbound to their call.

How weak they are, she thought. She grinned at the befogged looks on their wretched faces and laughed at their impending doom. They walked on, blind to their own destruction, powerless to stop it and powerless to save their own lives as blood dripped from their ears and poured from their mouths; they were choking on it, sputtering, unable to scream at the horrors around them. Ursula thought it was the most beautiful and thrilling thing she had ever beheld.

If the sea witch had let the sirens' chorus continue, it would have brought death to the humans. But letting them die was too easy, wasn't it? She wanted to see their terror and watch them suffer. She wanted them to become the thing they feared and hated most.

She wanted them to show their loathsomeness.

As her hate penetrated Ipswich, she was surrounded by wrecked lands as far as she could see. She stood within the landscape like a shining thing of beauty among the ruin, her face pale from rage, her eyes mournful but brimming with revenge. Her heart full of hate.

Divine hatred.

That was what it was.

Divine.

She felt truly alive for the first time. She felt no pity for them as she watched them bleed; there was no hesitation on Ursula's part, and she had no time for pleading or crying. They had been silenced by the song of the sirens. They stood before her, sickly and foul, watching in silent horror as Ursula led them to their destruction.

"The power of the old gods, I call you to me,
the Deep Ones, to claim these humans for the sea!"

With this spell the humans fell to the ground, convulsing, struggling for air. They looked around, gasping, and saw their fellow villagers transform into horrific sea creatures. Now they were forever bound to Ursula, to do her bidding. Forever inhuman. Forever monstrous and vile.

Ursula's laugh swelled from her gut and sounded throughout the lands, reaching the ears of every witch in the many kingdoms. It sent a shiver through even the most powerful among them, dark and light, because they felt the weight of this. They knew the power of hate-infused magic and the destruction it could bring. The dark grey mists curled around Ursula as she watched the terrified humans struggle against their transformations, their silent screams making the scene more beautiful to her.

"Don't fight it, my darlings!" She laughed. "Or perhaps you should! It hurts more to struggle!"

This was far more rewarding than she had imagined. It was splendid, this hate, this utter destruction.

It was glorious.

Ursula's laugh thundered as she stepped into the encroaching waves at the shore, encouraging all her new creatures to journey into places unknown to them, dark places they had been too frightened even to contemplate. Places they had only visited in their nightmares or anxious, fevered daydreams.

The creatures were hers now, servants, and she would use them at her will and to their torment. As the waves touched her human feet, she slowly transformed. It seemed the creature within her had no choice other than to burst forth from the human flesh, desperate to be seen and aching to be in the waves.

She was growing to leviathan proportions now, towering over her terrified minions, bawling with laughter at their plight.

Then, unexpectedly, a figure emerged from the water, like the *Flying Dutchman* breaking the surface.

"Stop this lunacy at once!" The voice was louder than the crashing waves.

Whereas Ursula seemed nothing but darkness, he appeared like shining light. He was beautiful, too beautiful, and seemingly too good. Those were traits she found all too prevalent in males of higher rank in those lands. She had no idea who that minor god might be, but she already knew she didn't like him.

"Who are you to command me?" she asked, snapping her head to the right to get a better look at this mockery of the gods.

"Did you not call upon the old gods? I have answered."

"I called for help, not interference!"

"Look around you! Look what you've done to this land! Everything is scorched with your hatred. It is blighted as the lands of the old queen. Don't take her path, little sister. Come home with me, where you belong."

Ursula was silenced, perplexed.

"Hear me, Sister. See that necklace you are wearing? It was a gift from our father. We thought you were lost to us forever. I hoped one day you would come to know your power and call upon me, but I didn't expect to find this." His face was screwed up with a look of disgust as he surveyed the destruction Ursula had wrought.

"You know nothing of my life! I was left here alone with these humans who feared and hated me. You have no idea what I've suffered!"

"Ursula, do you truly not remember me? I am your brother. Triton."

Ursula looked at Triton, furious and confused. Unable to place him.

"I'm sorry, Ursula. It's time I brought you home."

CHAPTER I

THE SEA WITCH

It had been many years since Ursula had seen her dear friends the sister witches. Not since right after her exile from Triton's court had she paid them a visit. There was so much to catch up on and as she made her way, she saw light dancing across the rippling water and knew she was at last reaching the surface. She could almost make out the shadowy images of the three sisters standing on the shore, waiting for her arrival.

It has been a rather long time, she thought and decided she might as well make a grand entrance, with a great spectacle. She felt herself growing, her tentacles elongating, a sensation that always made her feel like the dominant force of the seas that she was.

I haven't felt this power within me for ages.

She'd taken down massive ships in that form, splintering them, casting their remains deep into her dark, foreboding realm. She saw the looks of astonishment in the odd sisters' bulging eyes as she rose out of the water to towering heights. The trio of sister witches, Lucinda, Ruby and Martha, looked small standing on the wet black rocks and shivering in the cold.

Ursula thought the sisters possessed a grotesque beauty, with their too-large eyes, tiny mouths and pale haunting faces that were framed far too perfectly by their raven ringlets. She found them beautiful even if the mists clinging to the feathers in their hair made them look like frightened, soggy, flightless birds.

One wouldn't know it by their frightful state, Ursula mused, but those witches were the things of legends. They were cousins to the old king, the father of the queen called Snow White. And they were great benefactors to the Dark Fairy and her sleeping princess. Though Ursula would never say so aloud, she owed her newly regained power to the odd sisters. They had returned her necklace. Although, she considered, it was a fair exchange for something their little sister had desperately wanted.

Lucinda gasped as water spilled from Ursula's massive form onto the witches' awestruck faces, their ears splitting with Ursula's thunderous laughter and booming voice.

"I'm so happy to see you, sisters. It's been far too long."

The sea witch leaned down to be at eye level with the odd sisters. They were really quite striking, she thought.

But too much beauty without the proper proportions.

Ursula's arms were outstretched, ready to embrace them. The sisters scuttled tentatively as one into Ursula's embrace, which eased their concern and relaxed them with the fact that Ursula was not cross with them.

"I see you are wearing our gift," said the sisters

in unison, spotting the golden seashell necklace round her neck. All were worried Ursula would be enraged if she ever learned it had been stashed away in their pantry half-forgotten all that time.

Ursula laughed, this time at the sound of the sisters' scratchy voices and at the state of the drooping feathers in their pitch-black hair.

"Thank you, my dear friends. You will have to tell me how you got it back from my brother at some point. Or was it Circe? I didn't ask her when she brought it to me. And where is Circe? I'm surprised she isn't with you."

Circe.

The mention of her name was like knives being plunged into the odd sisters' hearts. She had been a source of heartbreak for them, the reason Lucinda had called on Ursula for help. Circe was the reason the odd sisters cried endlessly, vainly crying her name into the darkness, hoping she would at last return on account of their pleas for forgiveness. Circe hadn't answered her sisters' calls, so they summoned the sea witch for help. Of course, Ursula would want something in return. She always did.

She was the maker of deals.

Lucinda spoke first. "Circe, our beloved, has gone far from us…" Her deep red satin gown was stained with tears, and like her sisters', her eyes were smudged with black coal makeup that had streamed down her cheeks from long hours of crying.

"She's so angry with us! She's ventured where our magic cannot follow," continued Ruby.

Martha's sobs were almost too violent for her to speak. "That's why we've come to you, Ursula. We want to see our little sister again."

Ursula asked the obvious question: "Have you tried to summon her, dears? In one of your many enchanted mirrors?"

The sisters broke down crying again.

"She must have done a spell when she left that keeps us from summoning her!" Martha's sad bulging eyes, which were so much like her sisters', were filled with grief and fear.

Ursula could tell they were truly afraid. She couldn't recall ever seeing her friends in such a state, so full of regret and so grief-stricken. "I promise you, Martha, I will help you find Circe. I promise each of you, my dearies, you will see your little sister again."

Then Ursula smiled one of her magnificent grins, which slowly transformed into something a bit more mundane as she used her magic to assume human form and took the sobbing Martha into her arms. She knew the sisters would give anything to see Circe again, and as much as she wanted to help them, and *of course* she would be happy to do so, *she just so happened* to be in need of the odd sisters' special brand of magic in return for her favour.

CHAPTER II

THE WITCHES ON
THE CLIFF

The dark green gingerbread-style mansion with gold trim and black shutters was perched precariously on the rocky cliffs. Its roof, shaped like a witch's cap, was obscured in mist and encircled by screeching crows.

"Is the Dark Fairy to join us?" asked Ursula as the four witches made their way to the odd sisters' home.

"No! No! Water and fire do not mix!" said Lucinda as Ursula laughed. Ursula wondered why the sister witches so feared a convergence between her and the Dark Fairy.

"We fear nothing, Ursula, but we see and hear

everything," Lucinda said casually, giving her the side-eye as they headed up the crooked staircase, which creaked with every step.

Ursula mused over the many locations in which she'd visited the house. She wondered if it grew chicken-like legs and moved on its own steam or if the sisters just conjured it wherever they desired. Surely it was simply summoned, but she loved the image of the sisters riding in their witch's-cap house powered by giant leathery chicken legs, the witches cackling within the entire way. The thought made her laugh as they entered the queer little house in which she'd so often been a guest. The location might have changed often, but the house, with its quaint little kitchen, remained the same.

The sun shone through a large round window on the main wall that looked out over the old queen's apple tree and the waves crashing onto the rocks. The shelves were filled with beautiful teacups in differing patterns, as if collected from various sets. Ursula wouldn't be surprised if the sisters simply slipped cups they fancied into their handbags. She wondered if each cup had a unique story, the story of its owner and of its encounter with the dreaded sisters three.

Which of those cups, Ursula wondered, belonged to the old queen, or to the horrible sisters Anastasia and Drizella? And which belonged to Maleficent?

Off the kitchen was the main room with a large fireplace. Its mantel was imposing and flanked by two enormous ravens that gazed out into the nothingness with steely eyes. The room had an eerie light, coloured by the stained glass windows with images of the witches' various adventures. One of the windows had a simple red apple. It was lonely and sad, Ursula thought, but perhaps that was because she had heard the old queen's tale from the sisters many years before.

How many stories had she been told sitting near that fire when she deigned to take human form? That human form, that creature, she thought, it wasn't at all to her liking. She felt small and weak when hiding in her human shell. Her voice also sounded different - not as booming or demanding. There was no power in it.

No majesty.

She couldn't fathom how humans had survived as long as they had in those weak sacks of flesh, always in pain, always walking or sitting on hard furniture. It was horrible, that human nonsense.

At least she had Lucinda, Ruby, Martha and their charming cat, Pflanze, to distract her from the pains of being human. Pflanze, the sisters' tortoise-shell cat, blinked her black-rimmed golden eyes slowly at the witches in salutation.

"Hello, Pflanze," Ursula said, smiling. Pflanze adjusted her paws and blinked again, welcoming Ursula to her home. Pflanze could see through the sea witch's human form to the creature she really was. And the cat thought that creature was even more beautiful than the form the sea witch had taken so she could walk among humans.

Oh, it was beautiful enough, Ursula's human guise. She had large dark eyes and full deep brown hair that framed her heart-shaped face. Anyone would find her beautiful, but Pflanze loved the sea witch's true design, and it was easy to see the witch preferred it as well.

Pflanze watched as her witches scuttled about the kitchen getting the tea ready for Ursula, who had her feet propped on a little cushioned stool Ruby had brought for her. Pflanze's witches had been quite unlike themselves since their little sister, Circe, had left, and Pflanze was growing worried they would wither from their constant fretting. But what troubled the cat more was how quiet the sisters had become. She was used to their insane ramblings and manic chatter. But now the house was almost unbearably quiet without Circe to fawn over. Now the sisters would simply sit and mope, uninspired even to cause their usual mayhem. And when they spoke, they did so as coherently as they could manage, in an attempt to make their sister Circe happy when she finally came home. Pflanze presumed that if the sisters had hearts within their hollow, hateful shells, they had been broken the day the witches' little sister left with hate in her eyes, anger in her words and a deep sadness in her heart.

Circe wasn't like her sisters, Pflanze mused. She loved. And Circe felt Lucinda, Ruby and Martha had finally gone too far with their magic, hurting someone she had once cared for very deeply. Pflanze didn't blame the sisters for what they had done to the Prince, the curse they had helped set on him or the torments they had rained upon his head. They had almost driven him mad, and with good reason. He had broken Circe's heart and treated her rather shabbily.

Everything they had done, all the meddling and scheming, was for their little sister. But Circe was terribly angry with them for the part they had played in the curse, which had sent the Prince further into his greedy, hurtful ways, nearly destroying kingdoms in the process.

No, Circe couldn't forgive her sisters, and Pflanze was almost sure she would never speak to them again as their punishment. The beautiful feline hoped the visit from Ursula would inspire a wee bit of wickedness and bring her mistresses out of the deep depression they'd been suffering.

But Pflanze's musings were shattered by screams that caused Martha to drop the glass teapot, breaking it into tiny shards on the black and white kitchen floor. Ruby was sobbing. The glass sparkled like diamonds, dazzling in Ursula's eyes. Soon Ruby's sobs were so severe she found herself in Ursula's arms as the sea witch tried to calm her theatrical ravings.

"Pflanze thinks Circe will never speak to us again!" Soon all the sisters were screaming and crying, wringing their hands and ripping their dresses. Martha started pulling her hair, and Lucinda was ripping at the feathers in hers, casting them about the room like a madwoman.

"Ladies, stop!" boomed Ursula's voice, and the sisters could see, cast onto the wall behind the elegant human body Ursula was hiding in, the shadow of her true form, dominating the kitchen.

"Silence!" Ursula commanded.

The sisters fell quiet.

"You *will* see your little sister again, I promise you, but first there is something I will need from you."

CHAPTER III

WITCHES IN IPSWICH

The witches were standing on the rocky cliffs, looking down on the small coastal town of Ipswich. Its little weather-worn cottages were barely distinguishable under the thick layer of soot. You could feel the hate emanating from the place, the pain and suffering that were not only inflicted but that imbued the magic that caused this nightmare.

The sisters were not only intrigued; they were impressed.

Like all witches in the land, they had felt the shudder of power when Ursula caused that ruination so many years before. The place stood like a monument to death, a reminder not to cross the sea witch. To the sisters, it was beautiful.

Even Ursula's brother could not cleanse that land. As pure as his magic was, it could not penetrate Ursula's hate. Not even the old queen's rage had caused that much destruction. Oh, she, too, had blighted the lands, but she had left one singular tree with a shiny red apple, a symbol of the tiny shard of hope and, indeed, love that remained within the Wicked Queen's dark and lonely heart.

That was the old queen's failing, the sisters thought: her love. She had never truly relinquished herself to grief and anger. She had never completely filled her heart with hatred. Even now the old queen looked in on her daughter, Snow White, stealing glimpses of her in an enchanted mirror, the sisters' mirror! The thought of it filled the sisters with rage. Snow White still had one of their treasures and was therefore protected by the old queen and forever out of the sisters' reach.

The old queen had failed them so miserably, allowing herself to be swallowed by grief, loneliness and fear, and ultimately weakened by love. Even in death, she surrounded Snow White with her everlasting love and protection. The sisters often wondered what the old queen could have accomplished if she hadn't destroyed herself for the love of her daughter. She was such a bitter disappointment. But Ursula was different. There was no one to distract her, no one for her to love. She was alone in the world, alone in her grief and alone with her pain. No, she wouldn't disappoint them. Unlike the old queen, Ursula would be able to fill her heart with hate.

Oh, but the Beast, he had been close to doing that, hadn't he? Too close, they thought. He'd had a hate within him that sometimes frightened even the sisters. If it hadn't been for Circe and Belle, he would have died of his hateful, greedy ways.

Their thoughts returned to Ursula and how powerfully distinct she was from their other subjects. She was a remarkable creature and a magnificent witch with none of those human failings. Her hate was righteous and pure and untainted by self-doubt or conscience. There weren't many witches like Ursula, and the odd sisters were happy to call her their friend. But why had she brought them there?

What was that place to them?

Unlike the odd sisters, Ursula was not privy to others' thoughts. The sisters sometimes forgot that and then remembered they needed to use their voices if they expected to get answers to their questions.

"Why this town?" "Yes, why? There are so many towns like it." "Towns filled with murderous fishermen." "Why take revenge on this one?"

Ursula laughed gutturally at the simplicity of their scope. She hadn't waged war on the human town because its residents offended the sea. It was much more personal.

"This was my home, dear sisters. This is where it began, and I want to share my story." Ursula paused, lost in thought, and then continued. "We're here because I want you to help me kill Triton."

The witches shivered. Magic fuelled by hate was very powerful indeed. And if Ursula was willing to gather all their hate, which was their impression, then there was a chance they could destroy Triton, but the sisters needed a reason. They needed to be invested. They needed to hear her story.

Hate, *true* hate, wasn't just conjured; it was birthed. It had to come from within so it might become its own entity and slither into the hearts of its enemies to choke them. If this was a truly worthy cause, if their hate could be harnessed, there was nothing the witches couldn't destroy. Then the sisters thought of her.

Their Circe.

Her heart was full of hate, probably for the first time. She harboured hatred for her older sisters deep within her beautiful little heart, a heart they had thought was too full of love to hold hate for anyone, especially her family. Never even in their wildest of frenzies had they ever considered the possibility of losing their little sister's love. It didn't seem possible, but it was true: she detested them for their foul meddling with that damnable Beast! No matter how the odd sisters pleaded, Circe wouldn't listen to reason. Her heart was broken, shattered into tiny pieces, and Lucinda, Ruby and Martha couldn't mend it.

Circe's magic could keep her from her older sisters for an eternity if she chose. At once, the thought sent chills down the odd sisters' spines. Never to see their little sister would be the worst of punishments, the most horrible thing they could imagine. And they wondered if they deserved it. Surely Circe was making more of things than she should. Everything they had done was for her. In defence of her. For the love of her. All for Circe. All for their dearest little sister. They would happily risk their lives to destroy the sea god Triton if it meant they could see her again.

They would destroy anything. And with stakes like those, they knew it wouldn't be too difficult to muster their hate.

Chapter IV

The Little Sea Poppet

Tucked away in the gingerbread-style mansion, Pflanze and her witches prepared for Ursula's story. The sisters put Ursula in their most comfortable spot next to the fireplace, in a lovely overstuffed periwinkle velvet chair with many red quilted pillows piled high to rest her weary feet upon. She was not used to walking on land, on two legs, and it wore on her.

Alongside her chair was a little round table with a rose-patterned teacup set on it. Steam curled up and out of the cup like wispy tentacles. If it hadn't been for the unfortunate events for both the sisters and their dear friend, this would have been just like one of their countless delightful visits during which they'd usually gossip about the goings-on in the various kingdoms or share stories of their wicked deeds. There was nothing quite like sharing stories with other witches, especially with a witch like Ursula.

She was a true witch with a royal background and with great power, but most important, she had a sense of humour. There was nothing she didn't find humourous, even in herself. She was the cheekiest witch they knew, and that was probably why their little sister, Circe, liked her so well.

Oh, Circe.

Their dearest little sister. Would they ever see her again? Was she lost to them forever? "What if something terrible happened to her?" cried Ruby.

"You must stop this obsessive fretting over Circe at once, Ruby, please!" "Yes, calm yourself. Ursula is going to share her story now."

Ursula's voice was calm and flat. There was no hint of her customary histrionic flair. Her voice did not boom. It was almost small, and she seemed more serious than the sisters had ever seen her.

"My father found me floating on the waves, clutching to a piece of splintered wood, which he presumed was the tattered remains of a terrible shipwreck. He scooped me out of the sea and brought me back to his village and that is where I lived.

"With my father.

"He called me his little sea poppet and raised me as his daughter. And that is what I was: his daughter. I waved him goodbye every morning when he went out on his fishing boat, and prayed the sea gods would bring him back to me safely, which they always did. He was the only person in the world who truly loved me. He thanked the sea gods daily for bringing me into his lonely life, and I thanked them for bringing him into mine. Neither of us could know of the thing growing inside me, the power I had, or the form I would eventually take. If only I had trusted in his love and confided in him when I started to fear the thing I was becoming."

The sisters were listening intently. Waiting. Waiting for the rage and fury. But Ursula had fallen silent, lost, it seemed, in her own thoughts. Memories, no doubt, of her father. They had never seen Ursula so pensive.

Martha broke the silence. "Did he betray you? Men always do, don't they? Fathers never love their daughters as they should!"

Ursula shot Martha an icy stare but didn't answer.

"Was he revolted by your aquatic form? Frightened of your power?" "Oh, I bet he tried to kill you! Fathers are always a disappointment!" "Oh, we can help with hateful fathers!" "We can call upon the old queen if you don't believe us!" "If only Snow White didn't have the mirror!" "Oh, we know a thing or two about wicked fathers!"

Through unexpected tears Ursula simply said, "No," and the sisters knew they had got it wrong, terribly wrong, and they immediately regretted their words.

They fell silent, waiting for their friend to answer, even though they already knew it wasn't her father at all; it was the people of the village.

"It was *them*, wasn't it?" Ruby muttered bitterly. "It was those wretched villagers!" Pflanze narrowed her eyes and adjusted her paws. She had very little affection for most humans. They had always proven to be distrustful and full of superstitious notions.

"When I started to show signs of being other than human, I was frightened. I had no idea what was happening to me. I was afraid I had offended the sea gods in some way and they had set an affliction upon me."

"But you are a sea goddess of the highest rank!" the sisters chimed.

"I had no way of knowing that then. I was just a girl. Every day the sea's call grew more powerful and the urge to leave my father's shores harder to resist. The village was full of simple-minded fools, all of them too willing to blame every little mishap on the gods. All of them pointing fingers at those who may have brought the gods' fury upon them. All except my father, who had managed to keep to himself until I came into his life."

Poor Unfortunate Soul

Pflanze thought her witches might cry, seeing the salty tears well up in Ursula's eyes and realising what must have become of her father. What a terrible way to learn she wasn't of this world.

Inevitable, but terrible.

"I walked to the cliffs every morning after my father went out on his boat. There I looked to the sea for answers, wondering why I felt this way, why I felt different from those around me, and why I felt compelled to dive off the cliffs. I thought I must have been going mad, and I feared there was something terribly wrong with me, because surely I would die if I were to jump into the sea. That I should want to end my life in such a horrible way caused me great terror, but somehow deep within me I sensed death wouldn't be waiting for me in those cold, dark waters.

"It was something else, something familiar yet far too frightening to discover. I knew in my heart if I succumbed, the ocean would claim me in some other way, and to me that was like a sort of death, to be away from my father, who loved me so dearly.

Every day I stood there, willing myself not to jump, praying to the sea gods to give me strength to stay ashore, but one foggy morning I could no longer resist the urge and I jumped. And what I discovered was frightening beyond all imagination."

"Is that when they discovered you?" asked Lucinda, her eye makeup smeared from crying.

"Yes, they were waiting for me on the shore. They dragged me to the centre of town, where they were going to burn me. These were people I had known my whole life and they were coming out of their homes and piling anything that would burn onto my pyre."

"How did you escape?" Ruby asked.

"My father drove most of them off with his harpoon, threatening to kill them if they didn't let me go, but soon there were too many..."

She was quiet again, clearly caught in the nightmare from her past.

"They ripped him to shreds, my father, trying to get at me. Trying to put me back on the pyre. He put himself between us, giving me the chance to escape, and I did, into Triton's realm."

Lucinda spoke. "Triton's realm, you say! By rights it is yours, as well! You are his sister!"

Ursula sighed. "I didn't know who I was then. Triton didn't make himself known to me until I blighted Ipswich.

"He is no brother of mine. He didn't care what those foul humans did to my father! What they did to me! Oh, he brought me to his kingdom and presented me as his beloved sister, but even he wouldn't let me live among his people in my true form!"

She stood from her chair, knocking over the pillows, clenching her fists and raising her voice in anger. "This was the face that greeted my new family! And this body, with the exception of a mermaid's appendage! He didn't think his precious merfolk could stomach the likes of my true design, so he ordered me to hide myself within a mermaid's body!" she continued. "He didn't want *me* as a sister! He wanted *this*!" Pflanze understood. Triton *had* stolen her beauty. He made her hide in a version of her human form, not allowing her to be herself. She had been trapped and made to feel loathsome.

What a sorry brother Triton was, the cat thought. What a terrible brother indeed. Lucinda and Martha listened, fearful of saying something out of turn, but Ruby, as she often did, went against her sisters' wishes. "You are a very powerful witch and can take any form you like! What does it matter which one you choose?"

"What does it matter?" Ursula yelled, her body now growing taller and more expansive. "What does it matter?" Very rarely did Ursula show her true self while on land. It was painful and made it difficult to breathe, and in the wrong company was possibly very hazardous to her well-being. But for just a moment, just the slightest of moments, she let herself be revealed, as if the anger within her could no longer be contained.

"You're right! I *can* take any form I like! *This* is how I choose to look, and I have nothing to be ashamed of!"

"Of course you don't!" sputtered Martha, clearly

in awe of Ursula's rage.

"But that wasn't the worst of his misdeeds, my darlings! Remember, I was in that village for years and my brother never came looking for me! It wasn't until after my father was killed and I returned to destroy those foul murdering humans that he made himself known to me! And why? Why do you think he came? Not because he loved me! Not because he had been searching for his lost beloved little sister! He sought me out because he couldn't rightfully take the throne without proving I was dead or unworthy! He abandoned his baby sister and didn't bother looking for me until it served his aims! I think he used his magic to bring me into my powers so I would transform among those who would hurt me. He must have known I was among humans and how they would react. That they would try to kill me! I would be surprised if that wasn't his goal. His actions caused my father's death and he felt nothing for my loss of him! You know how Triton feels about humans. He wouldn't have bothered with condemning me for what I did in Ipswich if the humans hadn't been transformed and sent to besmirch his realm, to soil his precious kingdom with human hybrids!

"You should have heard the tales I learned while I was at court! Stories of Triton's wrath brought down upon humans who offended the sea were legendary! Why, then, would my actions be so offensive to him, do you think, if not to set me up as some madwoman, some evil, vile murdering creature unfit to share his throne? When things were at their worst between us, when he was still making a pretense of wanting me to be by his side, he actually said my father deserved his fate for the countless murders he committed as a fisherman, and for not fearing the gods."

"Deserved to be torn to shreds by those horrid humans? Your father was protecting you!"

"Triton cast me aside because he feared my power!" Ursula said. "He said he was appalled by what I did to Ipswich, but truly I think he was afraid I would do the same to his kingdom and take it by force!"

She continued, growing more enraged.

"I don't think he ever intended to accept me as his sister, and I didn't know why he insisted I come back to his kingdom as such. We fought endlessly, and our arguments have become things of fables only the bravest of his subjects retell. Do you know he has banned all mention of me in court? The youngest of his daughters don't even know I exist, and the eldest was told her memory of me was a nightmare. *He brought me there simply to prove I was unworthy to share the throne.*"

"You could have ruled together!" said Lucinda, feeling Ursula's sorrow for the loss of her father and possibly for the loss of her brother, as well.

"And now, instead, I shall take his kingdom, *my kingdom*, by force and destroy anyone who stands in my way! He could have been my brother, my family, but that time has passed! Damn him to Hades for what he's done. Damn him to nothingness!"

And there it was.

Hate.

Hate for the foul human creatures who had

murdered Ursula's father and for her brother, who had treated it like a trifling matter. Hate for the brother who made his sister feel like a loathsome creature to be shut away and never looked upon.

The sisters gathered that hate like a precious gift, because that was what it was. It was the very thing that was going to bring them the power to return their sister Circe to them. Now they just needed to devise a way to kill Triton. Ursula smiled another one of her wicked grins. It was the sort that made you certain she was conjuring a plan. And she did indeed have a plan...

"We will ruin his daughter." She laughed.

Lucinda cocked her head to the right. "Which daughter? There are so many!"

"The youngest, my precious creatures! Isn't it divine?"

Ruby twitched with delight and rubbed her hands together. "Princess Ariel?"

"Yes, my dears! She's made it quite easy for us, actually."

"Has she now?" asked Martha while casting her

eyes about the room, looking for Pflanze, who must have slunk her way out of the witches' company without their notice.

"Yes, my darlings! It's delicious! She's fallen in love with a human."

"A human? A human!" squealed Ruby. Martha and Lucinda chimed in.

"What do you think dear old daddy will make of that?" Ursula smiled. "His hatred of humans is legendary! He brings down their ships at every opportunity." The sisters looked at each other in a way Ursula had grown to understand after being so close with them for so many years. They had an idea. "What is it, my darlings? What have you concocted in your devious little minds?"

The sisters sat silently for a moment in contemplation, their large eyes widening and smiles growing, cracking the facade of their smooth white porcelain faces and causing them to look like crumbling whitewashed stone. "She will want to become human herself." "It will kill Triton! Turning his beloved daughter into something he loathes."

"But that isn't enough! It's just one of his many punishments." "First to see her transformed, then witnessing her destruction!" "Only then will he understand true loss."

Ursula laughed and said, "But not before he surrenders his soul. And that, my dearest darling witches, will be his undoing." With that all the witches laughed, delighted in their hate and with their scheme. This time, however, they were sure not to allow their voices to travel to the kingdoms beyond, as was customary.

This was a dark, secret sort of magic, and they couldn't stand for interference of any sort, not even from a well-meaning witch who wanted to lend her magic to their mix. No, this was far too important, because their hate was pure. Their righteousness was unpolluted by doubt.

"We will ruin Ariel; the daughter will pay for the sins of the father. And then we will kill Triton! And when we do, we will *dance*!" "Yes, dance! We will dance on the grave of your tyrant brother!" The three sisters spun in circles, dancing around

Ursula, who had splendidly transformed into her true form. Her tentacles grew and curled around the odd sisters as they stomped their tiny black boots, singing songs of Triton's death while Ursula's laugh rattled the teacups and potion bottles in the little house where the witches plotted the ruin of Triton's youngest daughter.

Ariel.

CHAPTER V

THE VISITOR

Morningstar Castle stood high upon the rocky cliffs, overlooking the ocean like a brilliant lighthouse in the fog. The castle was, in fact, built upon the remains of a cyclopean lighthouse, left from days when giants had ruled those lands after their great battle with the Tree Lords.

Within the ancient lighthouse was a magnificent lens, fashioned by a crafty dwarf by the name of Fresnel. The lens resembled a giant crystal jewel and it cast a brilliant light that guided the ships safely away from the rocky cliffs. The castle was intentionally built not to look dissimilar from the original lighthouse; it was fashioned with gloriously cut windows so the lights within would also function as beacons.

But to see Morningstar Castle properly, to truly experience its beauty, one must see it on solstice from a distance while traversing the sea. Sailors and fishermen would journey out of their way, sometimes by tremendous distances, just to see the castle, referred to by most as the Lighthouse of the Gods. The Morningstar clan was a well-respected family, always willing to help those in need, and of course they were great friends to those who sailed the perilous seas, often giving aid to anyone who washed up on their shores shipwrecked or lost their way on long journeys. Indeed, they were one of the few royal families without enemies, and they genuinely got on well with the other kingdoms they encountered. But their closest allies were the kingdoms under the seas, for they depended on the sea gods for their well-being.

King Morningstar had long before made an agreement with the sea witch who dwelled in those waters that he wouldn't interfere with her kingdom.

And she, in turn, wouldn't meddle with his. Unlike her brother, who detested humans for fishing his seas, Ursula was rather more relaxed on the matter, as long as the Morningstars' fishermen stayed within the specified boundaries. And those boundaries were within Ursula's domain, the Unprotected Waters; her brother had no jurisdiction there. The agreement was to everyone's benefit, and while the Morningstars held to their portion, the sea witch saw no reason to break hers. So she hadn't broken their agreement when she found the king's daughter, Princess Tulip, after she had thrown herself off her father's rocky cliffs. She was, after all, under the sea and in Ursula's domain, and the princess was all too eager to take Ursula's deal: her beauty and voice in exchange for her life.

When Tulip looked back on that terrible experience, it was as if it were another lifetime. She was looking back now as she curled up on the window bench of the sunny morning room, drinking her tea, with Ursula's distant voice ringing in her ears: *"Well, well, my dear. Are we so brokenhearted as that? Is the loss of that terrible prince really worth your life?"*

"No! I've made a terrible mistake."

"Yes, you have, my sweet, but I can help you. There are just two things I will need in exchange: your beauty and your voice!"

Tulip was happy to fling her beauty away. It was the very thing that had caused her such misery. It seemed no one except for her beloved Nanny ever considered Tulip's other attributes. The Beast prince loved Tulip only for how her beauty could reflect upon him. She was expected to sit idly, always looking beautiful and saying nothing, while he did what he willed. And she had filled the role remarkably. She cringed thinking about what a fool she had made of herself in those months, horrified she had allowed the Prince to treat her so shabbily. That was what beauty had brought her. Heartbreak. Humiliation. And without it, without her beauty, Tulip could focus on what made her herself. Life meant so much more to her than she had ever realised. And her voice, well, it had got her into nothing but trouble. She was happy to be rid of it, happy not to have to make small talk, or frankly to have to talk at all.

After that day by the sea, she had decided to be done with the business of being a princess. No more fancy balls or being carted off to meet men of royalty. Certainly no more engagements to awful cads! Her parents begged her to reconsider the idea of a good marriage, and she almost relented out of guilt. As much as she wanted to help her father's kingdom by marrying some wealthy prince, she couldn't fathom another terrible brutish man in her life. No! She wouldn't allow it!

She had set her mind quite firmly on the matter and decided she liked her life exactly as it was, when an enchanting young woman named Circe came to negotiate with the sea witch for the return of Tulip's beauty.

"But I don't want it! I don't want to be beautiful!" Tulip screamed. Circe was beside herself. She almost regretted having convinced Ursula to return Tulip's voice just moments before.

"But, my dear, it belongs to you. It's yours.

I've got something for the sea witch that she will want much more than your beauty, and I daresay you won't have much choice in the matter. The deal is sealed, as they say. She may not have the item until your beauty is returned, and I guarantee Ursula would destroy the entire pantheon to get at it."

Much to Tulip's horror, she was once again beautiful by the next morning. It was like some sort of twisted fairy tale, all confused and backwards. You see, once Tulip had her beauty back and this Circe girl had seen to it that Tulip would be in possession of a wealthy dowry, every prince from every kingdom was travelling to Morningstar Castle to ask for Tulip's hand in marriage. Once, Tulip would have delighted in being fawned over, but she was now eager to dismiss the vile and pathetic men who did the fawning.

Tulip was content to spend her days sitting with her nanny or reading books from her library. She had grown used to the way life had been in those days before Circe's visit, the silence of the room as she read about adventurous, brave young women escaping their terrible stepmothers or the Dark Fairy who put a spell on a young girl for her own protection.

She had liked not having to speak, and for the first time, she had truly spent time with herself, not worrying about impressing this prince or that, or wondering if she'd said the wrong thing at dinner or worn the shade of pink that best brought out the colour in her cheeks. She'd never felt happier in her life, or more content.

Nanny brought her out of her thoughts when she padded into the room. "What's this, Nanny?" Tulip asked, looking at the basket Nanny was holding. It was bedecked with a bunch of pretty pink roses that looked fearfully familiar.

"Well, I don't know, child! But it's clearly from that loathsome kingdom." Nanny was speaking, of course, of the ghastly prince to whom Tulip had once been engaged. They had heard he had since changed his ways and fallen in love with a remarkable young woman named Belle. Apparently they were very much in love and were living quite happily together.

Tulip found that hard to believe, based on how the Prince had treated her. But she also recalled meeting Belle at the Prince's ball and noted to herself that she wasn't the sort of woman who would stand to be mistreated. If anyone could bring about a change within the Prince, it would be a woman who could stand up for herself in a way Tulip never could.

She hoped they were happy together, the Prince and Belle, and she appreciated the letter the Prince had sent to her shortly after his marriage, begging Tulip for her forgiveness and promising to make things right with her father. She quite frankly couldn't imagine the Prince writing such a letter and was surprised when her father later shared the news that the Prince had indeed made good on his word. As gallant as his recent actions had been, she couldn't banish from her mind or heart the foul things he had done to her, and she decided it was best to avoid any further correspondence with the lout.

"You don't think it's from *him*, do you?" Tulip's lip was quivering at the mere thought of that nasty beast she had almost married.

"I shouldn't think so, dear! Perhaps it's from old Mrs Potts. She was awfully fond of you."

Princess Tulip laughed at her nanny's calling anyone "old Mrs" *anything*. Her nanny, whom she loved deeply, was impossibly old and resembled a withered apple doll, with her shrivelled and heavily lined powdery white skin and her brilliant silver hair. She was short, shrunken with age and slightly stooped but with a fierce personality and a spark in her eye.

"Open it, my dear! Open it up!" Tulip looked at the package suspiciously and decided to open it as gingerly as she could, fearful there might be something dangerous inside. But she was happily surprised.

"Pflanze! My dear girl, I missed you!" Pflanze was a beautiful black, white and orange cat the princess had grown to love during her stays with the Prince when they had been engaged. Sometimes the cat had been her only company while the Prince had gone off to the tavern to drink with

Gaston, leaving her alone and weary at his every opportunity. She had mourned the loss of Pflanze's companionship in the many long months since all that wickedness had transpired with the Prince. But as she had mused earlier, that was a lifetime before.

She sometimes looked back at herself, feeling stupid and foolish for having allowed the Prince to treat her as he had. *Well, that will never happen again!* she thought as she petted Pflanze. Lately she'd made it her business to learn something of the world. No more fumbling for the right word or giggling rather than taking part in a conversation. She was a new woman and she'd never been happier.

"Oh, Nanny! It's my Pflanze!" Tulip squealed.

"I don't like it, my girl! Not one bit! I won't have anything from that accursed place in our home!" Pflanze gave Nanny a terrible look. But she knew that Nanny wasn't like most humans; she saw things others did not. Pflanze wouldn't be surprised if Tulip's dear nanny was a witch who had lost her powers and memories long before but had an inkling of magic still within her.

"Nanny, no! It isn't Pflanze's fault! And you know very well the castle is no longer enchanted! Circe told us so on her last visit."

Pflanze's ears perked up. That was why she had gone there. She was hoping for some news of Circe. She didn't doubt her witches' power or ability to find their little sister, and she knew they were in fine company with Ursula, sequestered away with their schemes, potions and spells. But Pflanze wanted to help, and since Morningstar Castle was the last place Circe had visited before she took to paths unknown, Pflanze thought it was a good place to start.

"I don't care if he's married to the sweetest, most angelic girl in the world! I still don't trust him!" Nanny bellowed, clearly still angry with the Beast prince.

Ignoring her nanny, Tulip turned her attention to her long-lost friend.

"My goodness, Pflanze! How did you get here?" The silent beauty looked at Tulip with her black-rimmed golden eyes but couldn't answer. Pflanze hoped that Tulip assumed she had been sent to her by someone at the castle. The princess didn't know Pflanze belonged to the odd sisters, of course, or who the odd sisters were, for that matter. Tulip had always assumed Pflanze lived in the court of the Beast prince (and so she had, for a time, when it suited her mistresses).

"Can't we keep her, Nanny? You know how much I love her! I've often spoken about it."

Pflanze rubbed her face against Tulip's and purred.

"I suppose, my dear," Nanny sighed, unable to deny her Tulip almost anything. "But perhaps we will have Circe take a look at her and make sure she was not sent for evil means!"

"My goodness, Nanny, the way you talk! You'd think Circe was some sort of witch that could do such things!"

"Well, she is, my dear! A truer witch than I have ever met!"

"Nonsense, Nanny! I won't have that sort of talk! Circe is a dear friend! Like a sister!"

Nanny sighed. "Well, when she visits next, it

wouldn't hurt to ask what she thinks. Do you know if we're expecting her soon?"

"She comes as she wishes, but it's been some time. Last she was here she was trying to explain the virtues of trust and opening up to the idea of falling in love and all that rubbish again. As if I'd marry one of the arrogant fools who have been clamouring at the gates since the return of my beauty and fortune! I'd rather spend my days reading and learning something of the world! Not trapped away in some man's castle, at his beck and call!"

Nanny smiled at Tulip knowingly. "Well, my dear, that is the last thing I want for you, as well. But perhaps now you will find a young man who loves you not only for your beauty and fortune but for your enchanting mind."

Tulip wrinkled her nose in distaste, but Nanny continued.

"And if you do, my dear, I wouldn't be so quick to turn my nose up at him!" Nanny put her hand on Tulip's cheek tenderly and looked deep into her sky-blue eyes. "I daresay whether you had lost your beauty or not, you would have realised your potential. You forget, Nanny sees into your heart, and she always knew there was an eager mind waiting to be filled with knowledge. Your beauty wasn't holding you back, my love, you were. I'm so happy you've found yourself at last."

Pflanze thought Nanny was right: her old friend Tulip had rather changed... and she liked it. She had never minded Tulip's silly, dim-witted nature; she had always found Tulip quite sweet and loved the attention she heaped upon her. But this new Tulip with a sense of self was interesting, and Pflanze could tell she was going to enjoy Tulip's, and indeed Nanny's, company more than ever.

CHAPTER VI

POOR UNFORTUNATE SOULS

Deep within the ocean, below the cliffs of Morningstar Kingdom, was Ursula's lair. It was fashioned out of the skeletal remains of a horrid sea monster and it glowed with an eerie putrescence. The sea witch was happy to be home with her minions and the comfort of all her things around her. She had recently spent far too much time on land and needed the tranquillity of being under the sea. The three sisters had their tasks on land and were working hard at them while Ursula prepared below for her visit from Triton's youngest daughter. There was only one element of the spell they required.

Ariel's soul.

Ursula's pets were swimming about her, having missed their mistress desperately when she was away with Lucinda, Ruby and Martha. But they were careful not to speak just yet, for they knew she was devising her schemes to trick Ariel. They watched their mistress with a shared enthusiasm, each with a sickly yellow eye glowing in Ursula's murky domain. Only Ursula knew the true nature of the beasts, but they seemed to inhabit the same mind, making them appear symbiotic in their deviousness.

The slinking creatures sliced through the water and Ursula watched through a mystical bubble in her throne room as Ariel rushed home to Triton. The little mermaid was late for the most important event of her young life, her presentation to the merfolk.

"Yes, hurry home, Princess, we wouldn't want to miss dear old daddy's celebration, would we? Celebration indeed! Bah! In my day, we had fantastical feasts when I lived in the palace. And now, look at me... banished and exiled! While he and his flimsy fish folks celebrate! Well, I'll give them something to celebrate soon enough.

"Flotsam! Jetsam! I want you to keep an extra close watch on this pretty little daughter of his. She may be the key to Triton's undoing..."

How Ursula hated being relegated to these paltry dealings since being banished from her brother's kingdom and sent off into the darkness to usher little exchanges for bits of power. It would have taken an eternity to steal one soul at a time, waiting until she had enough power to destroy Triton. If it hadn't been for the odd sisters and their dear sister Circe's returning the shell necklace Triton had previously robbed her of, Ursula wouldn't be in full possession of her powers.

It played in her favour, however, to let her brother think she was still powerless and alone in the darkness with only her harmless spells, not that they were ever really harmless, mind you, just not as grand as they might have been.

Until now.

She smiled when she looked upon the withered little souls in her garden, the poor unfortunate creatures she'd taken into her charge. It wasn't her fault they flitted their lives away. No one had *made* them place their souls in her hands; they were the ones unable to fulfill the terms of the contract, not her!

Now that she had her true powers, she needed not meddle in the lives of Triton's silly subjects. She needed not lure them into the unprotected realms seeking her magic, hoping she would fulfill their wishes in exchange for their souls. She had real power now, her own. And she had great allies in the sisters. If she was going to take a soul, it would be for her pleasure and amusement. Yes, she only had to play the part of the maker of deals one last time. After that, she needed not ever put herself on display like a carnival barker, singing her wares, enchanting her would-be victims with songs about her desire to help those in need. It was sickening, really, the depths to which she'd had to sink to gather the pitiful little souls in her garden. Those days were finally behind her. She had only one more performance. One last soul she needed for bartering purposes.

Ariel's.

She wondered what the girl was like. It was difficult to tell from the glimpses she caught in her bubble orb. She was no doubt headstrong like her father. That could mean she would drive a hard bargain. The girl was beautiful, too. Ursula couldn't imagine Triton having a daughter who wasn't. He certainly couldn't stand to have a sister who didn't fit his image of beauty. Then Ursula thought of *her:* Athena, Ariel's departed mother. She had been very beautiful, even for a mermaid. Ursula wondered if Ariel shared her mother's heart as well as her beauty.

Remembering Athena made Ursula's heart hurt. *Ariel isn't Triton's daughter alone,* she thought. *She shares her mother's blood, as well.* Would Ursula be able to destroy Athena's daughter? Athena had fought endlessly with Triton, defending Ursula, trying to persuade him to let his sister rule by his side, reminding him of their parents' wishes. The memories felt hidden, as if they were veiled by murky water or a thick fog, hard to reach, hard to connect to, because Ursula was no longer the creature who cared what her brother thought of her. Athena had never made her feel loathsome. Never made her feel ashamed of who she was. Never wanted her to hide. If it hadn't been for Athena, Ursula would have gone off into the Unprotected Waters long before she was banished. It was Athena who had railed against Triton the night of ball, denouncing his treatment of his sister when she had decided to show up to the royal function in her true form. It was Athena who had called her beautiful. And Ursula believed her words were heartfelt and true.

But she couldn't think of Athena. She couldn't be distracted by the past. She needed Ariel's soul. *If she is anything like her remarkable mother,* Ursula thought, *this girl should be willing to fight for what she believes in, even against her father.* But there was only one question worth asking: *Is Ariel the sort of girl willing to wager her soul for the possibility of true love?*

"Well, well, we shall see!"

CHAPTER VII

THE WITCH'S LAIR

After only a few days, far sooner than expected, Ursula heard stirring at the entry to her lair, shaped from the gaping maw of a sea creature's skeleton. She turned to see Ariel following close behind Flotsam and Jetsam, just beyond the sharp teeth of the entranceway.

She chuckled at the wide-eyed beauty trembling in the darkness with her red hair floating in Ophelian fashion. *Too fitting*, Ursula thought as she laughed again. She had to admit this daughter of Triton's was a lovely little creature with her large blue eyes and bunny-like features. She looked remarkably like her mother, and it almost made

Ursula sad to scheme against the near mirror image of the only person in Triton's kingdom who had treated her with the tiniest shred of kindness and respect.

"This way," Flotsam and Jetsam hissed, and Ariel shuddered.

The poor dear was struggling in the garden of lost souls. If she'd had any sense about her, she would have escaped then, but luckily for Ursula, the minds of young girls with rebellion in their hearts were easy targets for the likes of the sea witch. Triton had caused his own undoing when he drove his daughter away by destroying her collection of human trinkets and condemning her for loving a human. Well, her aunt Ursula would take pity on the poor girl. She would take her to her breast and give her a chance to snare that handsome prince she had fallen in love with so she might leave her tyrannical father behind... alone, to be snatched by Ursula, who would then gain her rightful place as queen.

"Come in. Come in, my child. We mustn't

lurk in doorways. It's *rude*! One *might* question your upbringing!"

Ursula laughed as she swam to her mirror to touch up her makeup and add a bit of flair and drama to the conversation.

"Now then, you're here because you have a thing for this human, this Sir Prince fellow? Not that I blame you. He is quite a catch, isn't he?" Ursula laughed as Ariel listened, transfixed by the sea witch.

"Well, angelfish, the solution to your problem is simple."

Taking a page from the odd sisters' beauty book, she slathered on a brilliant layer of red lipstick. She pursed her lips and kissed them together to smooth the lipstick. Then she finished her thought.

"The only way to get what you want is to become a human yourself."

"Can you do that?" asked the frightened mermaid.

"My dear sweet child, that's what I *do*! It's what I *live for*. To help unfortunate merfolk, like *yourself*. Poor souls with no one else to turn to..."

She hated performing and the way it made her feel. But she found it was the very best way to get her victims' attention, to entrance them with a spectacle they couldn't resist. And she did love the opportunity for a bit of cheek!

"I admit that in the past I've been *nasty*. They weren't kidding when they called me, well, a *witch*! But you'll find that nowadays I've mended all my ways, repented, seen the light, and made a switch! *True? Yes!* And I fortunately know a little magic. It's a talent that I always have possessed. And here lately, please don't laugh, I use it on behalf of the miserable, lonely and depressed."

Hardly able to stomach her own words, she whispered to her minions, *"Pathetic!*

"Poor unfortunate souls! In *pain*, in *need!* This one longing to be thinner, that one wants to get the girl and do I help them? Yes, indeed!

"Those poor unfortunate souls! So sad, so true! They come flocking to my cauldron, crying, *'Spells, Ursula, please!'* and I help them! Yes, I do!

"Now, it's happened once or twice someone

couldn't pay the price, and I'm afraid I had to rake 'em across the coals.

"Yes, I've had the odd complaint, but on the whole I've been a *saint* to those *poor unfortunate souls!*

"Now, here's the deal. I will make you a potion that will turn you into a human for three days. Got that? *Three days!* Now listen, this is important! Before the sun sets on the third day, you've got to get dear old princey to fall in love with you. That is, he's got to kiss you. Not just any kiss, the Kiss of True Love! If he does kiss you before the sun sets on the third day, you'll remain human, *permanently*, but if he doesn't, you turn back into a mermaid and... you belong to me!"

Ariel looked stunned.

"Have we got a deal?" Ursula asked.

"If I become human, I'll never be with my father or sisters again."

"That's right, but you'll have your man. Life's full of tough choices, isn't it? Oh, and there is one more thing. We haven't discussed the subject of payment. You can't get something for nothing, you know!"

"But I don't have..." said Ariel.

Before she could finish, Ursula interrupted. "I'm not asking much, just a token, really, a trifle! You'll never even miss it. What I want from you is... *your voice.*"

"My *voice?*"

"You've got it, sweet cakes! No more talking, singing... zip."

"But without my voice, how can I..."

"You'll have *your looks*! *Your pretty face!* And don't underestimate the importance of *body language!* The men up there don't like a lot of blabber. They think a girl who gossips is a bore. Yes, on land, it's much preferred for ladies not to say a word. And after all, dear, what is idle prattle for? Come on, they're not all that impressed with conversation. True gentlemen avoid it when they can. But they dote and swoon and fawn on the lady who's withdrawn. It's she who holds her tongue who gets a man!

"Come on, you poor unfortunate soul! Go ahead! Make your choice! I'm a very busy woman and I haven't got

all day! It won't cost much... just... your... voice! You poor unfortunate soul, it's sad but true: if you want to cross a bridge, my sweet, you've got to pay the toll. Take a gulp and take a breath. And go ahead and sign the scroll!"

Ariel closed her eyes and signed the scroll, flinching from Ursula's power. The moment she finished she knew she had made a mistake.

A terrible mistake.

What have I done?

The scroll was signed and tight in Ursula's fist and quickly conjured away with her magic. Ariel wondered if she would be able to make the prince fall in love with her, and if she did, would her father ever forgive her? Was this boy she hardly knew worth it, giving up her family, her home... her *voice*? She felt as if she were floating in a nightmare, in this hideous place, surrounded by revolting creatures and Ursula's daunting voice as she said the magical words that would bind their contract:

"Beluga, sevruga, come winds of the Caspian Sea!

"Larynxes, glossitis, et max laryngitis, la voce to me!"

Ariel wanted to scream, "No! Stop! I've changed my mind!" but where would she go? Home to her father, who had destroyed everything she'd loved when he blasted away her most prized possessions from the surface world? Her father, who had forbidden her ever to see her prince, Eric? No, Ursula was right. She had no other choice.

The sea witch's cauldron, which she had been filling with ghastly ingredients collected for this purpose, was exploding with blue light that swirled around them like a menacing wall. Ariel's heart was pounding, thundering in her ears, and she felt a deep sorrow for betraying her family and, worse, for betraying herself. She knew her father would never forgive this. She knew he would never love her again.

Ursula laughed.

He will hate you, as he hates me! He hates all things different from himself, little angelfish. The swirling light transformed into large groping hands greedy for Ariel's voice.

"Now *sing!*" Ursula commanded.

The gruesome hands grabbed at Ariel's throat, starting to take from her the thing that most made her who she was: her voice. The sensation was terrifying. It hadn't occurred to Ariel that losing her voice would be so painful. It was like a separate entity struggling to remain within her, and Ursula was literally tearing it from her throat, from her soul. The pain was terrible. She tried to let it go willingly, to stop struggling, but she couldn't. Everything within her fought against the assault. And then it happened.

Her beautiful, beautiful voice, it flowed from her lips involuntarily.

"Keep singing!" Ursula screamed, and her laugh was heard throughout the many kingdoms as her cauldron cast a golden light that surrounded Ariel, ripping her merbody asunder, turning the mermaid into the thing her father hated most: a human.

A human under the sea.

It wasn't Ursula's concern that the girl could no longer breathe underwater. *She will need to find a way to the surface. Or not.*

POOR UNFORTUNATE SOUL

CHAPTER VIII

NANNY'S SECRET

It had been several weeks since Pflanze had arrived at Morningstar Castle, and everything she'd heard on the day of her arrival was true. She and Tulip were up in the king's highest tower, looking down on all of Tulip's "gentlemen callers," as Nanny liked to say. There were at least five and forty of them, all waiting for the slightest glimpse of Tulip. The guardsmen had gone out more than once to get the young men to stop fighting with each other, reminding them all that the princess would not care for brutish men who brawled like common drunkards at the local tavern.

It didn't seem to help matters. The men kept

vying for Tulip's attention, some of them in more unique ways than others. One of the men, for example, stood out from the rest. He was wearing a sky-blue velvet frock coat with gold embellishments on his lapels and white lace ruffles at his sleeves and cravat. He played a lute decorated with lovely matching ribbons, which he used to compose songs about Tulip's beauty.

"Her skin is like honey, her eyes like the sky. Her hair is like sunshine—"

Tulip slammed the window before she could hear the rest of the song.

"This is just too much, Nanny! Really! It's getting rather ludicrous, don't you think?" she asked, frustrated with the endless parade of suitors.

"It really is, my dear! What possesses them?" She quickly caught herself and added, "Not that your beauty shouldn't command such attention, my dear!"

Tulip sighed. "I wish I knew. It's like a mania! Something has come over these men and taken hold of their senses! I'd feel sorry for them if it weren't so… annoying!"

"I agree, my dear! I think we should call upon Circe!"

"Call her? How do you suppose we do that?"

"I have my ways, my dear! You just leave it to old Nanny and Miss Pflanze here."

Pflanze gave Nanny a puzzled look and let out an inquisitive meow, wondering what the old woman had in mind.

"Pflanze? What do you want with her?" Tulip asked. "You get queerer every day, Nanny!" Nanny gave Tulip a kiss on the cheek as she scooped up Pflanze and took her off to their mysterious errand.

"Come on, my dear girl. I should like your company for a while."

It wasn't customary by any means for Nanny to be down in the kitchens, searching for this thing or that. And it was clear the chef was rather put out when Nanny suggested he take a nice afternoon walk.

"You're looking a little peaky, dear. You really

should spend more time in the sun. It will do you some good to get out and about. Perhaps a walk?"

The chef grumbled, leaving the little cakes he had lined up to decorate sitting on the marble counter, not wanting to argue with Nanny.

Nanny set out a saucer of heavy cream for Pflanze while she got a few things together. Pflanze knew at once what she was up to. Nanny intended to do a scrying spell. Pflanze had seen her witches do it many times in the years she'd spent with them. She heard Nanny in the pantry muttering to herself while gathering the herbs she needed.

"Everyone thinks Nanny is a silly old woman, but she knows a trick or two." Pflanze watched Nanny break an egg into a wooden bowl. It floated on the surface of the water like a strange eye, but that's what it was, wasn't it, an eye? A way to see into the world. The sisters had already tried finding Circe that way, but perhaps Nanny's magic would find her where the sisters' could not. Pflanze was pleased that she was right about Nanny's being a witch.

"That's right, precious!" Nanny said to Pflanze, who was leisurely drinking her cream. "And I know who you belong to! But never mind that now. They don't meddle with the likes of me. Not anymore. Not after our dealings with the Dark Fairy." Pflanze wondered for the briefest of moments if Nanny could read her thoughts, but she decided the old woman was simply talking to herself as she often did, and as she continued to do then. "It's time to find their little sister, Circe. We need to know what's come over these men! Clearly they're enchanted and it's not by your witches. It's someone else's magic and I don't like it one bit!"

Pflanze didn't blink an eye at Nanny's mention of knowing her mistresses. Other witches didn't frighten her, especially sweet elderly witches who'd lost most of their powers. Hopefully Nanny would remember the proper incantation to call up Circe. Pflanze knew it, of course, but had no means of conveying it to Nanny - not any that she intended to use, anyway. Not unless Nanny really *could* read her thoughts. Pflanze's magic was unlike the witches'.

It took long stretches of time to recharge. It sometimes took Pflanze years to recover after using her magic, so she had to choose very carefully the precise time in which to employ it.

Nanny gave Pflanze a funny look, like she knew what she was thinking, and it made Pflanze wonder... "Oh, yes, precious kitty, I can hear you! Old Nanny isn't as batty as everyone thinks! Give me the spell, girl! It won't cost you anything to think!" Pflanze wondered if Nanny had been skilfully hiding her powers all that time, or if they'd recently been coming back to her.

"Ever since you arrived, dear, they've been coming back to me like the divine winds! I suppose I should thank you."

You're welcome, Pflanze thought. Then, because she had learned to conceal her thoughts from her witches long before, she thought to herself, quite secretly, mind you, that this was a very curious situation, one that needed some attention and investigation. Clearly Nanny had been growing more powerful by the moment, and somehow

Pflanze was the cause, but even more important, Nanny remembered some dealings with the cat's mistresses and the Dark Fairy, whom her witches seemed to fear, but she couldn't think of that right then. She needed to focus on finding Circe, not only to make her witches happy but to see if she had any part in the spell that had overtaken all the young lads camped out on King Morningstar's castle grounds. It did seem like Circe's magic, that was the sort of thing she would do, try to bring about a match for Tulip, but it was getting out of hand; it wasn't like Circe to let her magic run amuck, and that was what bothered Pflanze most. If Circe had cast the spell, she would know its outcome and she would come at once to mend things. Unless something was detaining her...

"Yes, my precious! My thoughts exactly! I'm worried Circe may be in trouble, as well!" The old woman and the cat's conversation was interrupted by the clamour of a couple of castle guards running into the kitchen. The scene was rather ridiculous really, the men standing there wide-eyed, looking at

Nanny and Pflanze, wondering what to make of an old woman chatting with a cat while clearly in the middle of some witchery. It was remarkable that one man was able to bark out their orders.

"Up… to the tower at once!" he stammered.

"Here now, young man, I won't have you, or anyone, ordering me to towers, or to anywhere else, for that matter!"

"Excuse me, mum, but the queen commands it! The castle is under siege!"

CHAPTER IX

THE DARK FAIRY'S WARNING

The Dark Fairy's crow was perched in the apple tree outside the witches' gingerbread mansion. It looked at the odd sisters, who were whispering in their kitchen. From the expressions on their faces, the crow could see they didn't find his mistress's message at all pleasant.

"Do you think she knows?" hissed Ruby.

"She knows something! Why else send the warning?" Lucinda was incensed. "And who is she to warn us? She who meddles in the lives of children!"

Martha gasped. "We're not to speak of the child, Lucinda, not ever! We made a promise!"

"And so we have, but I won't have Maleficent interfering with our aims! We must find Circe!"

Ruby was ripping her dress, as she always did when anxious. Bits of red cloth littered the black and white kitchen floor like splotches of blood.

"Maybe we should ask her for help. Make an exchange. If we agree to sever our pact with Ursula, the Dark Fairy will have to help us find Circe!"

"No! We cannot betray the sea witch or there will be a price. Likely far worse than any Maleficent could dole out!" said Lucinda. "And stop ruining your dress, Ruby, please! You look frightful."

"Maleficent is an ally, too!" said Ruby, looking at the state of her beautiful red dress, which was now in shreds. "What are we to do? What are we to do?" she asked, pacing the floor.

Lucinda was furious with her old friend and went out to the cliffs to speak to the crow. She made an effort to speak clearly and in a straight line, as Circe would call it, so there would be no mistake in the translation when he took the message to Maleficent.

"You tell your mistress to keep her foul screeching

creatures away from our home! We need none of her nasty spies about us! Do you understand?"

The crow snapped at Lucinda, but she knew the creature had no real power to harm her.

"Our business is our own, and if Maleficent wants our continued support, she will stop sending threatening messages, no matter how well intentioned she thinks they may be! We appreciate and value her friendship, as ever, but we will not submit to her demands!"

With a violent caw, the raven flew off into the mists, away from the sisters, to the land of fairies and the sleeping princess.

"Do you think you should have been so harsh, Lucinda?" asked Ruby.

"I don't fear Maleficent! Her powers are no stronger than ours! And by no means are they stronger than Circe's," said Lucinda.

Ruby wasn't convinced. "I wonder! She did know what we were up to even though we were careful."

Lucinda rolled her bulbous eyes at her sister. "We didn't think of the crows!"

Ruby pressed on. "But what if Maleficent is right? What if we *can't* trust Ursula? Ursula has always been our friend! She has no reason to betray us! But neither has Maleficent! It's all so confounding."

"Not really, my dear sisters," Lucinda replied. "The Dark Fairy has never had any love for Ursula. It's like I said: water and fire don't mix."

CHAPTER X

CALLERS AT
THE GATE

Princess Tulip's gentlemen callers had caused the sequester of the entire Morningstar household in the highest tower; the ladies were at the mercy of the guards' protection while King Morningstar was away on diplomatic matters. The young man in the sky-blue velvet and white lace, who they learned was Prince Popinjay from two kingdoms over, was shouting orders to the other young men, who had a battering ram and were attempting to break down the gates.

"Crash the gates, good men! To my bride! We shall take the castle by force!"

"Good gods! Did you hear that? They're getting

in! You, over there, push that case against the wall!"
Queen Morningstar was in quite a state, which
wasn't her custom; she had never been one to let
her emotions get the best of her. But now she was
shaking as she pointed out the large piece of wooden
furniture for the guard to shift. Tulip turned away
from the mayhem and towards her mother.

"Mother, please! No one is getting in! Please sit
down and calm yourself."

"Princess Tulip! Princess Tulip!" the men
chanted. "Princess Tulip! Princess Tulip! Princess
Tulip! Princess Tulip! Princess Tulip! Princess
Tulip! Princess Tulip! Princess Tulip! Princess Tulip!
Princess Tulip!" Over and over and over.

"Do you hear that? What's come over them?
They're going to hurt my baby girl!" Tulip's mother
was clutching her handkerchief, eyes wide with
terror. "Darling, please come away from the window,
come over here with your mama."

Ignoring her mother, Tulip turned her attention
to her nanny. "This is madness! Were you able to get
a message to Circe?" she whispered to Nanny.

"No, my dear, we were brought up here before we could."

Tulip was frightened, truly frightened for the first time since she had been in the Beast prince's company.

"Nanny, please do something!" she shouted.

"Come on, Pflanze, we have no choice but to do it here." Nanny went to the desk, got out three candles, and placed them on the floor. With a piece of chalk she drew a sign of conjuration within the triangular configuration.

"What's going on over there? What are you up to?" cried Queen Morningstar. "Some sort of devilry? Stop it! Stop it at once, I say!" Nanny casually waved her hand in the queen's direction, not taking her attention away from her task, and simply said, "Calm," putting Queen Morningstar into a deep sleep.

"Nanny! What have you done to Mother?" Tulip shouted.

"Hush now, girl, and let me do my work!"

Nanny and Pflanze stood before the place of

power and called Circe.

"We beseech the winds, fire and sea, bring us the witch, bring Circe to me!"

And in the candlelit triangle, they saw Circe's form, slight and wispy, translucent like pale smoke. She looked deeply frightened and worn from crying.

"Circe, my girl, what's happened? Where are you?" Nanny asked, but before the ghostly image could answer, a dark grey swirling mist entered the triangle, dispersing Circe's frightened image to places unseen. The mist was swirling around the room, starting to take the human form of a witch Pflanze knew very well.

Ursula!

Pflanze jumped onto the mantel and hid behind a large bust of King Morningstar; she wasn't quite ready for Ursula and her witches to know what she was up to. "So this is the famous witch of legend I've heard so much about? I'm surprised you were able to summon me on your own." Ursula laughed as she looked at Nanny.

"I was calling upon the little sister of the

dreaded three."

"I know very well who you were trying to summon. But I am the great sea witch, and you did call upon the 'winds, fire and sea'! Fool, you should know who I am. I *am* the sea!"

Nanny looked suspiciously at Ursula, who continued in the same fashion. "You should feel honoured I answered your summons! And yet I find you disappointed with my arrival! If you don't want my assistance, I am happy to leave and let you contend with the rabble at the gates all on your own."

"Of course we want your help!" Tulip interjected, looking more worried than Nanny had ever seen her.

"Well, angel cake, it looks like you've got yourself into a bit of trouble once again. What *shall* we do about it?" Even though Ursula was in her human form, she gesticulated and spoke in such a way that Tulip had no problem imagining the creature she had met under the crashing waves.

Nanny spoke before Tulip could. "We won't have any of your deals this time, Ursula! You keep your tentacles away from my Tulip!"

Ursula laughed.

"Calm yourself, old woman! She has nothing I want or need! I'm here out of pure charity! And these men are on *my shores* while your king is away and unable to protect his lands! If I take a payment for this deed, it shall be from him upon his return.

"Now, what to do about little Popinjay and his crew?" Ursula went to the window, casting her hands towards the crashing waves, which swelled to epic heights and smashed onto the castle gates.

"Yes, I think that will do very nicely." She laughed as the waves battered the men with a violent verve.

"Ursula, no! You're going to kill them!" screamed Tulip.

"What do you care for these fools?" asked Ursula, her laugh booming.

"Not a jot!" said Tulip. "But I don't want to see them die!"

"Then close your eyes, dear!" said Ursula,

laughing again, this time allowing her voice to echo throughout the lands, as was customary. She wanted no creature, no human or witch, to mistake who and where the power was coming from. Her voice was so piercing a flock of crows scattered from the nearby trees, screeching into the mists beyond.

"Damned birds!" she hissed as she toyed with the waves, making the men's bodies smash even harder against the castle walls. They were screaming in pain, bloodied and bruised, and begging the sea witch to stop their torment.

Pflanze looked on from her hiding place. Luckily for the cat, the king had an unusually large head (which, thankfully, Tulip had not inherited). As a result Ursula could not see Pflanze squinting at her from behind the king's bust. Pflanze didn't much care what happened to the men outside, but she was wondering what Ursula was up to.

"There! That will do!" Ursula said as she calmed the waves, leaving the badly injured men scattered on the castle grounds.

"Oh, yes, there's just one more thing. What, may

I ask, do you want with dear Circe?"

"It's none of your concern, Ursula," said Nanny, looking at the sea witch with suspicion.

"Oh, isn't it? What was your name again? Granny, was it? Well, it so happens I am helping Circe's sisters to find her, Granny."

"And we might have found her if you hadn't shown. I think..."

No, Nanny, no! Nanny looked about the room, trying to find Pflanze, whose voice was whispering in her head.

"You think what?" asked Ursula with narrowed eyes.

Say nothing, flatter her and make her leave. I don't think she can be trusted.

"I think we were very lucky you answered our summons. Thank you," said Nanny, taking Pflanze's advice.

"Yes, thank you, Ursula. We are again in your debt," Tulip repeated.

"Yes, my dear, you are. Well, at least your father is. I'll see to it those men no longer bother you, and please keep Granny here out of trouble. We can't have addle-brained old witches doing half-remembered spells all over the seaside. It can be dangerous, for everyone concerned. And please, leave the search for Circe to me and her sisters. If we need the help of elderly witches and dimwits, we'll be sure to let you know."

As unceremoniously as she had arrived, Ursula departed, leaving Nanny and Pflanze to wonder what the sea witch was up to and how she had known they were trying to summon Circe. Clearly they had to be more careful if they were going to reach out to Circe again.

Pflanze watched as Nanny took control of the situation. "Tulip, please see your mother to her room." Tulip began to protest. She wanted to ask what Nanny had done to her mother and what was going on, but Nanny didn't have time for explanations, not then. "Tulip, please just do what I say. Do you trust your nanny?" Tulip nodded, knowing there must be a good reason for Nanny's serious behaviour. "Then take your mother to her room and stay with her until she wakes." Tulip took her groggy mother up to her room while Nanny rang for Hudson, the head butler of Morningstar Castle.

"You rang, Nanny?" Hudson asked as he entered the room.

"Yes, Hudson, please see that Tulip is served her afternoon tea in her mother's room, and ask all the maids, upstairs and down, to gather as many candles as they can carry and bring them here to me."

It wasn't Hudson's place to question Nanny, but he was clearly puzzled. "Shall I ask the footmen to assist, mum?"

Nanny hadn't thought of them. "Yes, I need to infuse this room with as much light as possible, and I need to do it quickly."

"Of course, mum. I will take care of this right away." Hudson wasn't in the habit of interrupting his seniors, but he could tell whatever was the matter, it was important enough to panic Nanny. He hurried off to complete his tasks.

Pflanze hopped down from the mantel and squinted at Nanny. "Don't you go giving me the side-eye now, creature! You know exactly what I'm about to do!"

It didn't take long to get the furniture shifted and all the candles placed and lit, with Nanny orchestrating the scene like the greatest of maestros. The room was brilliant with light, and sitting at the centre were Nanny and Pflanze. They were encircled by many rings of candles, which seemed to go on infinitely when reflected in the many mirrors that adorned the room.

Pflanze had heard Lucinda say many times that fire and water did not mix, and she knew even without reading her mind what Nanny was up to. She was creating a wall of fire to keep Ursula from entering their magical circle again.

They were going to summon Circe, and this time Ursula wouldn't be able to interrupt.

Poor Unfortunate Soul

CHAPTER XI

THE ODD SISTERS' LAMENT

The odd sisters had spent far too much time fretting over the Dark Fairy's message, leaving Princess Ariel to find her way into Prince Eric's home by the sea. Luckily for the sisters, however, she hadn't found a way into his heart. Not yet. "We must focus all our attentions on Ariel," said Lucinda. "Where are Flotsam and Jetsam?"

"Oh! I'll get the mirror!" Martha shouted, scuttling off to find one of their enchanted mirrors so they could keep an eye on Ariel and the prince.

Ruby was shaking; she couldn't turn her mind from the Dark Fairy's warning. "Why did she have to send that message now, when we're trying to find Circe? Do you think she'll interfere?"

Ruby's endless fretting over Maleficent's message only succeeded in making Lucinda more infuriated with her old friend the Dark Fairy.

"I won't have her mentioned again, Ruby!" Trying to distract her sister, she continued: "Look, here is Martha with the mirror!"

"I have them! I have them!"

In the mirror Martha was struggling to drag into the room, the witches could see the images of Flotsam and Jetsam. The two creatures were spying on Ariel and Prince Eric.

"Someone help me!" Martha squealed, tripping on a snag in her tattered dress.

"Good gods, Martha! Why didn't you bring one of the smaller mirrors? Here, let me help you!"

The ladies successfully propped the mirror against one of the onyx raven statues that flanked the fireplace so that the sisters could warm themselves by the fire while spying on Triton's youngest daughter. Collectively they wondered if they were doing the right thing. A terrible sense of foreboding and anxiety was just under the surface, threatening to burst forth. They had been very careful not to fall into their old habits of interfering with others, casting harmful spells or even succumbing to their usual fits of lyrical mayhem. The sisters had in fact been rather subdued, and it was all for Circe. For their dearest little sister. They were even speaking normally, or doing so as much as they were capable, so their sister would accept them. She hated their odd rhyming speech. They wanted nothing more than to make her happy, make her proud of her older sisters. But wouldn't meddling in the affairs of Ariel and killing her father besmirch them further in their little sister's eyes? Surely it would.

But could they truly be certain? Perhaps it wouldn't bother Circe. In fact, they assured themselves, Circe might actually be pleased.

After all, Circe loved Ursula; she had said so herself. And if Circe knew the terrible things Ursula's brother, Triton, had done to her, not just the legends but the truly awful deeds, then she would help them.

How Triton had treated Ariel would be enough for Circe. She had no regard for fathers who kept their daughters from their true loves and destroyed their most cherished possessions. If Circe were there, she probably would have granted Ariel's wish to be human without payment, punishing Triton in the process. No, Circe wouldn't mind their schemes with Ursula. In fact, she'd probably help them.

"I don't think she would. She's too good," whispered Martha. "I don't think she'd like it at all."

Lucinda sighed. "We're doing it *for* Circe!"

Martha and Ruby weren't convinced. "But that is what we thought with the Beast prince!" "And now Circe is angry, refusing to see us!"

Lucinda was clenching her fists, willing herself not to unleash her fury on her sisters. "Ursula promises to help us find her! Once she has Triton's power there isn't much she won't be able to manage. Now, please, let's focus on helping Ursula."

"But isn't that what the Dark Fairy fears? Perhaps she is right? Should one witch have so much power?"

Lucinda grabbed a glass jar and threw it at the wall. It shattered, casting orange dust throughout the room with an explosion of fury.

"Do not speak of Maleficent again!"

Once over the shock, Ruby and Martha started screeching. "You've ruined the divination powder!" "Oh, Lucinda! You ruined everything!"

Lucinda rolled her large dark eyes at her sisters, wondering how she managed this long-suffering affair. "I've ruined nothing, you featherbrains. Martha has already conjured them in the mirror! We saw that as she entered the room."

The sisters mumbled in embarrassment and nonchalantly turned towards the mirror.

Within the mirror the sisters spied Flotsam and Jetsam swimming near Ariel and Eric's boat. "They're about to kiss!" squealed Ruby. "How could we have let this happen? Ursula is going to be furious!"

But before the witches could start screeching incantations, Ursula's devious slithering minions overturned Eric and Ariel's boat. The odd sisters sighed with relief while Flotsam and Jetsam gave each other mischievous grins, congratulating themselves for ruining the romantic scene.

"See? There is nothing to fear! Our distractions haven't led Ariel and Eric down the sickening path of love!"

"Not yet," said Ruby, who was clearly still distracted by other matters.

"What? What is it?" Ruby said nothing.

"Tell me!" Lucinda demanded.

Ruby, careful not to mention Maleficent's name, sputtered and twitched but managed to share her fears. "What if we can't trust Ursula? What if her story is lies? How do we know her brother truly did the things she said? And where is Pflanze? She's been missing since Ursula's visit!"

Where is Pflanze?

Pflanze. She was the last thing Lucinda needed to worry about now, what with the cryptic message from the Dark Fairy, Circe gone beyond their magic, and now her fretting sisters. Lucinda was full of rage but she could not place where it should be directed.

Should it be aimed at her sisters for questioning her authority? Or should it be at Maleficent for interfering in their plans to find their sister? Most troubling of all, she wondered if she was enraged at *herself* for blindly trusting Ursula.

Whatever the cause, it needed to stop. They couldn't go into their scheme with doubt or fear. She walked to the wall on which she had thrown the powder and gathered some from the floor, forgetting to be mindful of the broken glass. Her blood mingled with the orange powder, turning her hands a deep crimson, making her recall the Dark Fairy's warning: *Ariel's blood will be on your hands.*

She threw the powder she had gathered into the fire.

"Let us see times gone past when Triton and Ursula spoke last."

"That's not the correct metre, Lucinda!" hissed Ruby, who was very grateful Lucinda did not have the power to kill with a single look, because if she had, Ruby would have been lying on the floor, choking on her own blood.

"Silence, Ruby! I won't have you ruining this spell!" But she amended the lines just in case her sister was right.

"Let us see in times gone past when Triton and Ursula did speak last!"

She brushed the rest of the orange dust from her hands into the fire, conjuring Ursula in the flames. Ursula was on the shores of Morningstar Kingdom, saying her goodbye to Princess Tulip the day she had saved the poor girl from her sorrow and fear.

"Now, my little angel cake, I trust you won't go flinging yourself off any more cliffs for the love of a man who doesn't deserve you. And I daresay if another man does fall in love with you, you'll know he loves you for yourself and not how your beauty reflects upon him, and, my sweet cheeks, if that day comes, I will return to you your voice."

Tulip answered Ursula with a weak smile, and Ruby looked to her sisters, who were intently watching the scene. "This is the day Ursula saved Tulip from drowning after the Beast prince broke her heart. Where is Triton? We asked to see the last time brother and sister spoke, not this nonsense!"

Martha looked panicked. "I think you did the spell wrong, Lucinda. I told you the metre was off! This isn't even the right time period!"

Lucinda looked as though she might strangle her sisters. She could see herself taking their skinny little necks in her bony hands and squeezing the life from them.

"Well, that's a pretty scene you've conjured, Lucinda, I must say!"

Lucinda looked at Ruby as though she were a strange bug. "'I must say'? Since when do you say things like 'I must say'?" She scoffed and continued. "Sisters, please! I'm sure Triton will show eventually."

In the flames Ursula sighed as she watched Tulip walk the path that led to her father's castle; then the sea witch disappeared beneath the water. She actually felt bad for the poor little princess, not because she had lost her beauty, but because she had never truly appreciated it when she had it. Ursula was swimming home, feeling sullen, for her own losses as well as Tulip's, when a tightening grip seized her stomach at the sight of Triton's shell chariot outside her entrance. A deep anger swelled within her as she thought of him in her home. *How dare he enter without my permission!* He had often taken those liberties with her, not because they were kin, but because he saw it as his right. He had forsaken her long before, when he had banished her from his kingdom - not that he'd ever accepted her into his life during her time at the palace. He had never really tried to love her as a sister.

But that was a lifetime ago, she thought. Those days when she'd lived in his kingdom were like a faded nightmare now, hazy and out of reach. Now she lived in her own waters, the Unprotected Waters, far from Triton and his sycophantic subjects. Only the most desperate of those subjects came to Ursula's realm, and she was more than happy to oblige them.

Triton had painted her as a creature capable of only evil and wrongdoing. He would never dare admit that she had something to offer his people, despite the fact that together they could have ruled far better than either of them could alone. Surely that was what their mother and father had planned when they were alive. That was why they split their power between them, putting his into his trident and hers in the golden shell necklace Triton had taken from her when she was sent from his kingdom. He couldn't use her power even if he wanted to, not without her permission. Only she could wield her power, but he'd rather hoard it than let her have it, her rightful inheritance, and her rightful place at his side.

If she were able, she could reclaim that power, and with a little help from the sister witches, she might easily dethrone her brother. Lucinda, Ruby and Martha listened intently to Ursula's musings while watching her in the enchanted flames.

"Ah, there is the tyrant king," said Lucinda as the sisters watched Ursula slither into the gaping-maw entryway of her home. They heard the little cries and pleas for help from the creatures in her garden of lost souls. Ursula smiled at Harold. He had been the first of her victims and therefore with her the longest; she had come to look at him as one of her favourites. There was something about his sorrowful gaze that made her smile.

"Hello, Harold, my pet." She looked at all the souls she'd collected. "How are all my little darlings doing today?" She was trying to pretend she hadn't noticed her brother standing just beyond the garden.

"I see you've been keeping yourself busy, Ursula."

"I suppose you think you can enter any domain you choose, but I daresay you've overreached. You are, in fact, trespassing, sir!"

"I see the extent of your exile wasn't sufficient, Ursula. Clearly you are weaving your dark arts with those brave enough to venture into the unprotected realms and look upon your revolting visage."

Revolting visage.

Ursula choked back her pain, swallowed it and turned it into malice.

"Your subjects wouldn't come begging me for help if you didn't oppress them with your lunatic standards of beauty! Dear, sweet, lovable, stupid Harold here is a prime example. All he wanted was to impress the ladies with the virtues you and your court hold in such high esteem rather than being his dear sweet self, and look where it got him."

Triton tried to interrupt his sister. "Ursula..."

But Ursula kept talking.

"My contracts with your subjects are fair and binding. There is nothing your magic can do to help them, *Brother*."

"Do not call me Brother. You foul, murdering, ugly monster!"

Foul.

Murdering.

Ugly.

Monster.

That was what her brother had thought of her since the day they met on the shores of Ipswich. She wished she had memories of her brother from before that day. To imagine them young together only made her feel the loss of him more profoundly. Perhaps it was better to think their origins lay on the shores of Ipswich. There was nothing she could say or do to make him soften to her. He would always see her as a monster. No amount of love or support of his kingdom changed his view of her. Even when she hid within that false aquatic form he demanded of her, in the guise of what he deemed beautiful, she could sense him looking straight into her heart, which he saw as cold and black.

The way Ursula saw the town of Ipswich.

Ursula laughed.

"There was a time when your words hurt me beyond measure. Now they only fuel my hatred for you."

"You've violated the laws of the seas far too many times, Ursula. It's time you return to the shores so you can dwell with those pathetic humans you love so well!"

"Is this about the princess Morningstar?"

"Yes. You know the law. Her father's coffers have grown fat on fishing these waters! I won't have you protecting his children while he puts mine in danger every time his men cast their nets into the sea!"

"I am not bound by your laws, Triton. I do not live in your waters. This realm is mine! I make the laws in the Unprotected Waters! Besides, you might be happy to know his coffers are now empty after some bad dealings with the Beast prince. Perhaps that is punishment enough? I don't see why his daughter should suffer any further for her father's choices."

"Clearly you know well of daughters who've suffered for their fathers' choices."

"Don't you dare speak of my father! Not ever! You don't have the right!"

"That human wasn't your true father, and he deserved his fate for surrounding himself with those repugnant murdering humans! You've become the thing you hated, Ursula, just like your victims in Ipswich."

"Get out! And go back to your simpering, mealy-mouthed subjects! You have no power here, Triton! These are the Unprotected Waters. Your rule does not extend here or to me!"

"I have the means to take the last shreds of your

power, and I shall do so at my pleasure if you extend your support to another human. This is your final warning, Ursula. Keep to the shadows, where foul ugly creatures belong, so no one may suffer the sight of you!"

"If I am this foul creature you describe, it's by *your design!*"

"You've always been this way! You refused, even as a small child, to take the proper form."

She was thunderstruck. She couldn't believe what she was hearing. "What? What did you just say?"

"You heard me! You were a vile little thing. I left you adrift because I foresaw the monster you would become!"

"I wasn't lost as you said? You left me?"

"Yes, and clearly it was the right choice. Look at you. You're disgusting. Shameful."

Ursula thought she had hardened her heart against her brother long before, when he banished her from his kingdom, but this betrayal was more than she could comprehend. Her mind whirled at the notion of a young Triton abandoning his little sister to the perilous waves, not knowing if she lived or died. Hoping she had met the latter fate.

No wonder he had never sought her out all those years.

She hadn't the strength to ask what their parents had thought of her disappearance. She wouldn't be able to bear it if they had been privy to her brother's plan. Surely they hadn't. They must have been told some lurid tale of mishap. She wondered if they had ever suspected their "perfect" son of such a terrible deed. Why else would the king dictate that Triton prove she was dead or unworthy before he could take the throne? It was all too awful. Too profane. How dare he cast judgment on her when he had left his little sister to die? And to think that her parents might have been privy to his acts, that they could have known the truth. *That* would be too heartbreaking, too terrible even to fathom. It couldn't possibly be true.

She was done.

There was no love left for her brother. There was no doubt. And he had given her no choice. No

POOR UNFORTUNATE SOUL

choice at all. This foul, ugly, murdering creature was going to do what she did best. She was going to take her revenge.

CHAPTER XII

A SET OF STOLEN PIPES

Ursula didn't dismiss the near miss between Ariel and Eric as casually as the sisters three had. If it hadn't been for her poopsies' tipping over the boat, the prince would have kissed that little brat and it would have ruined her plans!

"Nice work, boys!" she said to Flotsam and Jetsam, looking into the magic divining sphere the sisters had given her when they saw each other last.

"That was a close one. Too close!" She was furious with the odd sisters for letting Ariel get so close to the prince. "The little tramp! Gods, she's better than I thought!" She was enraged.

"At this rate he'll be kissing her by sunset for sure." She swam to her pantry, where she kept all manner of components for spell craft.

What have those sisters been doing? I can't believe they allowed this to happen!

"Well! It's time Ursula took matters into her own tentacles!"

Smashing a glass ball containing a butterfly into her cauldron, she said, "Triton's daughter will be mine! Then I will make him writhe, and I will see him wiggle like a worm on a hook!"

All at once, everything turned gold, encompassing her, transforming her into... something else. Something she hated. *Vanessa,* she thought. *Revolting Vanessa, with its large violet eyes and long black hair.* She felt sickened in that human flesh, forced once again to use another's beauty to hide herself, but this would be the last time; of that she was sure.

As Ursula stood on the shores of Prince Eric's estate, wearing someone else's body, and carrying someone else's voice, she mused.

A Set of Stolen Pipes

Soon Triton would be dead, and she would take her rightful place on the throne. She would do so in her true design! How fortuitous that Triton's youngest daughter should fall in love with a human! How poetic! If she hadn't needed Ariel's soul, she would have let her marry Mr. Fancy Prince! It would have broken her father's heart seeing her become the thing he hated most. A human! It was divine intervention! But she had other plans for Ariel's soul. She wouldn't have bothered taking the little mermaid's voice had she intended the mergirl and Eric to marry.

The gods of fortune had been working in Ursula's favour the day the waves ripped Prince Eric's ship asunder, sending him deep within the ocean into Triton's domain. Thank the sea gods Ariel fell in love with Eric in that moment. Ursula's minions had told her when it happened. It was all too perfect: the gods granting the little mermaid the strength to save the prince and take him safely to shore! It was as if they were working towards Ursula's aims.

And as far as Ursula could surmise, the prince

had begun to fall in love with the gorgeous young redhead who had saved him, and he'd been pining for this dream girl ever since. Thank goodness she'd thought to take Ariel's voice or they probably would have married the moment she opened her stupid little mouth. The poor prince thought he'd conjured that songstress in his drowning delirium, the girl with the beautiful voice.

Now Ursula was in possession of that voice and she intended to use it; she intended to snare herself the little mermaid's prince and make him hers. Her musings were interrupted by the whistling sound of a human instrument, a flute, flying through the air and splashing into the waves.

He's here, she thought. *Perfect.* With Ariel's voice Vanessa sang the tune that had enchanted the prince on the day Ariel saved his life. She felt like one of her sirens: calling forth her prey, bewitching a human man with her song. Ariel's song. Drawing him to the shore and to his utter destruction. Then a thought came to her.

If she were to possess Triton's power and at

the same time rule in Eric's kingdom, she would dominate both land *and* sea!

It was too brilliant, too perfect and utterly divine. She would just need to keep Prince Eric enchanted as long as it served her aims. Then she'd get rid of him once he was no longer of use.

Eric wandered to the shore, drawn by the sound of Ariel's voice within Vanessa and bewitched by her magic. To say he had any thoughts or feelings of his own would be a great exaggeration. Or better, purely inaccurate.

It was a little unfair bewitching him like that, but Ursula didn't want to leave anything to chance. She could have simply lured him by employing Ariel's voice alone, without witchery, and he would have thought it was Vanessa who had saved his life, but time was running thin and she needed to be sure Eric wouldn't fall in love with Ariel. She needed Ariel's soul.

Had she any empathy left in her, she would have felt sorry for the poor prince, dizzy-eyed and befogged as he was. He seemed like a decent fellow:

quiet, sweet, humble. Rather moral… and far too handsome. When he approached Ursula in the fog, his eyes dazed by her magic, she sighed.

He finds this human shell beautiful. Not Ursula, he finds Vanessa *beautiful.*

She had never been loved for herself by anyone but the human who had adopted her. Her father. He had loved her even when she had transformed into something monstrous, ugly and foul, as her brother had called her.

Never mind the past! she thought. *None of that will matter. Not when both the land and sea are mine.*

CHAPTER XIII

PRINCE POPINJAY'S REGRET

Dearest Princess Tulip Morningstar,

*It is with deepest regret to you and your family
that I write you this missive. That I should behave
so dastardly is an utter mystery to me and leaves
me feeling quite ashamed. My only defence, a
poor one, is that I was quite unlike myself when
performing those actions. Indeed it felt as if I was
possessed by another and unable to enforce my own
will. I must assure you, madam, that actions such
as those are entirely out of my nature, all except
for my proclamations of love for you. (Though
I might have chosen a more suitable fashion to*

declare them.)

I must confess that I have loved you for some time. Ever since I saw you on the shores of your father's lands, coming forth from the sea like a silent mourning goddess, I have loved you, and I have watched you since as you've flourished into a strong, intelligent young woman. I had intended to present myself to your father's court in the proper manner, to be introduced officially, so you may consider a courtship, but I fear recent events have sullied your view of me. If that is the case, dear princess, I will not repudiate your feelings. I only want to bestow my deepest regrets and sincerest feelings of love and devotion to the most intriguing young woman I have ever had the pleasure of laying eyes upon.

Always at your service,
Prince Popinjay

Tulip sat gobsmacked, with the letter from Prince Popinjay in her hands.

She hadn't the words to tell Nanny what he had written - she hadn't fully processed what it meant - so she simply handed the letter over so Nanny might read it herself.

"Well, he is rather gifted at expressing himself! Better, I daresay, than he is at ramming down castle gates!"

Tulip was still in a daze. "Nanny, do you think what he says is true? Were those men under some sort of enchantment?"

Nanny knew very well they had been.

"Yes, my dear, they were."

Tulip looked at her sceptically. "Why didn't you say so before?"

Nanny sighed. "Because, my dear, you would have given me the look you're giving me now, like poor Nanny has lost her mind. And honestly, I had more pressing matters at hand, trying to summon Circe and contending with Ursula when she showed up in Circe's place. But trust me, my darling girl, those men were enchanted and your prince can hardly be held accountable for his actions."

Tulip's face squished up with displeasure.

"He's not my prince!"

Nanny laughed.

"If you say so, dear. But he sounds very much like your prince to me!"

Tulip hated this feeling. The last time she had felt this way, she had been utterly humiliated and deeply hurt. She couldn't imagine allowing herself to be charmed by another handsome man only to be heartbroken again. But she was different now, wasn't she? Stronger, bolder, and indeed more worldly. And it seemed those were the very qualities the prince admired in her.

"I wish Circe were here, Nanny. She'd know what I should do."

Nanny sighed. "I believe Circe would tell you to write this gentleman back, thank him for his kind words, and extend an invitation to tea."

Tulip smiled.

"Do you really think so?"

"I do, my dear."

"Then I think I will!" said Tulip with a quick

kiss for Nanny on her soft powdery cheek. Then she dashed out of the room so she might write the letter. Nanny laughed. How she had longed to see Tulip so happy again, and she felt Popinjay's intentions were honourable. But she'd better take a closer look at him just in case. *He's a fine fellow for a human,* said Pflanze in Nanny's head. *And I am sure Tulip will be quite happy with him, but we have to focus on Circe. I'm afraid she's in grave danger. I fear we all are.*

"I agree with you, Pflanze, and I think we both know who is behind it."

Poor Unfortunate Soul

CHAPTER XIV

HER ULTIMATE DESIGN

The kingdom was in a tizzy over the announcement of Prince Eric's wedding. The entire seaside was buzzing with excitement and a bit of confusion. Everyone was wondering who the young woman was, the dark-haired siren Prince Eric had fallen in love with.

Everyone, that is, except the little mermaid. When she heard the news of a wedding, the poor dear thought *she* would be marrying the prince. You couldn't blame her, really. They *had* almost kissed the day before, and something in his eyes when they were in that little boat together made her feel like... well, like he loved her. Maybe he finally remembered! Maybe he remembered it was she who had saved his life. She was so happy as she hastily tidied up before rushing to the landing to find Eric.

She had been fretting over how she was going to get him to kiss her before sundown, and now they would be kissing at their wedding! As she raced to the landing to find her fiancé, she saw something wholly unexpected, and it shattered her world and broke her heart.

The prince was standing with a beautiful young woman in the main hall, talking with his valet and great confidant, Sir Grimsby. Until that very moment, Grimsby had doubted the mysterious woman with the angelic voice Eric had been speaking of even existed. Grimsby had been haranguing Eric about his foolishness in pining for and swooning over a phantom siren when he had a lovely young woman beneath his very roof. But he had to admit Eric was right when he brought the young woman before him on that bright sunny morning.

"Well, now, Eric, it appears I was mistaken.

This mystery maiden of yours *does* in fact exist. She is lovely.

"Congratulations, my dear." Grimsby kissed Vanessa on the hand, welcoming her to the family.

"We wish to be married as soon as possible," said Eric in a hollow, enchanted voice.

"Yes, of course, Eric, but, ah, you see, these things *do* take time."

"This afternoon, Grimsby. The wedding ship departs at sunset."

Sunset.

Sunset!

The word sent terror through Ariel's broken heart. She saw the ruin of her entire life in that moment. Ursula's words echoed in her ears: *If he does kiss you* before the sun sets *on the third day, you'll remain human, permanently, but if he doesn't, you turn back into a mermaid and you belong to me!*

Ariel hadn't even thought about what that would mean.

Belonging to Ursula.

"Oh, very well, Eric, as you wish," said Grimsby

131

before hurrying off to make the preparations for the wedding.

Ariel was shattered.

She had lost her dearest love, and at sunset she would lose her soul to the sea witch. She would end up a shrivelled little creature in Ursula's garden and her father would never know what happened to her. She had made a ruin of her life with no thought for her family or her friends.

What would they think happened to her? Where did they think she was now? This wouldn't be happening if her father hadn't said all those awful things to her, condemning her for saving Eric.

His voice boomed like thunder in her mind as she remembered their horrible conversation. *Is it true you rescued a human from drowning? Contact between the human world and merworld is strictly forbidden!* She heard his voice as clearly as when he had said those terrible things. She had tried to make him understand, tried to make him see reason, but he didn't care. It didn't matter to him that Eric had almost died.

Her Ultimate Design

One less human to worry about!

It meant nothing to him that she loved him.

They're all the same! Spineless, savage, harpooning fish eaters incapable of any feeling!

It had only fuelled his fury, causing a cyclone of violence that had sent her seeking Ursula's help, help escaping her father and the life he wanted her to live, and it had all been for nothing. She would never know what it was to live in the human world. Her life was over before it had really begun.

She had been so foolish. Foolish to think Eric had fallen in love with her. Foolish to have made a deal with the sea witch. Foolish for throwing her life away for the love of someone who didn't love her in return.

She had been so sure Eric had fallen in love with her when she saved him from drowning. And he had taken her into his home when he found her on the shores of his kingdom. Why had she given her voice to the sea witch? If only he could hear her sing, he would know it was she who had saved him! She had thought for sure they were going to kiss in the boat the day before. She had thought he was starting to remember. She had thought he was falling in love. If only he had kissed her that day.

If only the boat hadn't turned over before... Never mind.

Her thoughts spiraled through the past few days, going over every detail, again and again. When her head stopped spinning, she felt nothing but regret. *I've lost everything!* she thought. *In three short days.*

She saw her dreams slipping away and turning into a nightmare. She had been so intrigued that night when she saw Eric on his ship playing the snarfblatt. She had never seen a human that close before, and she thought he was probably the most handsome being she had ever laid eyes on.

She had imagined what his life must be like, traversing the sea, seeing the world, dancing beneath the stars. She imagined where he must live, surrounded by beautiful things, human things, like those she had been collecting in her cave.

He could have shown her so many more human treasures, things she'd never even imagined. She had fancied her life with him as an endless adventure of discovery, and now it was all over.

She had thought the sea gods had brought this wonderful prince into her life for a reason, casting down his ship in that terrible storm. Plunging him into her ocean, giving her the means and strength to save him. Making her fall in love with him.

Why would the gods do that and not give them a chance at love?

She wouldn't have taken the risk if she hadn't thought they were meant for each other. If she had her voice, she could tell Eric everything! She was heartbroken and alone, wishing for the days when she first arrived in Eric's kingdom, when she thought he loved her. She couldn't believe he was about to marry someone else. She was helpless. She was desperate. And she was angry. She wanted to scream, but the sea witch had her voice.

"Ariel! Ariel!"

It was her friend Scuttle, the seagull. He flew onto the pier, rambling and in a panic. "I was flying, of course I was flying..." he sputtered, not making much sense.

Ariel could communicate with sea creatures, being one herself, and with the likes of Scuttle, but that didn't help her make out what he was saying as he sputtered and flubbed. Ariel desperately wanted to tell him to calm down and talk slowly as he continued, getting to his point at last.

"I saw the watch! The *witch*. The witch was watching the mirror and she was singing with a stolen set of pipes! Do you hear what I'm telling you? The prince is marrying the sea witch in disguise!"

Chapter XV

An Unexpected Message

The odd sisters' mansion sat against a brilliant pink, gold and silvery blue sky. The witches were within, peeking out their windows nervously, searching for crows, or any other sign from the Fairylands, fearful they would receive another odious warning from the Dark Fairy.

Ruby shrieked when she saw a dark grey owl flying towards the house.

"Stop, Ruby! It's just an owl!" But the sisters' stomachs started to twist in knots when they saw it was flying directly towards them.

"You don't think...?"

"No, I don't!" Lucinda snapped. "Maleficent

doesn't employ owls!"

Martha tentatively walked to the door, shaking with every step, glancing nervously at the stained glass window above their doorway, which was adorned with a deadly dragon destroying the Fairylands.

"Martha, please! Just open the door! The owl isn't going to breathe fire!"

When Martha opened the door, the owl swooped in, landed on the kitchen table, and stuck out its little foot.

"Ruby, give her a biscuit!" Lucinda ordered as she took the message from the owl's foot. Ruby and Martha searched through their various tins, trying to find the owl a biscuit, while Lucinda read the message.

"Stop all that clatter! It's from Pflanze! She wants us to come directly to Morningstar Castle. She says it's urgent!"

"What's the matter? Is she in danger?" Ruby and Martha were frazzled and Lucinda was doing her best to be patient with them.

"She doesn't say, just that she needs us and we will be welcome at court."

"I doubt that, Lucinda! Not after our role in Tulip's undoing!"

"Our what in Tulip's what? Since when do you speak like that?" Lucinda narrowed her eyes at her sisters, wondering what had become of them since they had driven away their little sister with their lunacy.

"We've all been speaking strangely since Circe left." "Yes, Lucinda, we agreed we'd try to speak more plainly for her sake."

The owl nipped Ruby on the hand to remind the sisters it was waiting for their reply.

"Ouch! I should snap your neck for that!"

The owl simply blinked its large globe-like eyes at Ruby as if to dare the witch to make good on her promise.

"Yes, yes! Hold on," said Lucinda, shoveling things from one end of her desk drawer to the other, looking for parchment and a pen with which to write her reply.

"Give her a biscuit!" she snapped while hastily composing her reply, letting Pflanze know they would be under way directly. "Tell her you're sorry! I won't have owls refusing to do our bidding, Ruby! We have far too many enemies already!

"Here, my dear," Lucinda said to the owl, attaching the message to its little leg and feeding it a biscuit. "Take this to Pflanze as quickly as you can." The owl gave a small hoot of thanks, finished the last of its biscuit, and flew out the round kitchen window past the old queen's apple tree and into the mists, towards Morningstar Kingdom.

"How shall we go, my sisters? The usual way?" asked Martha, who looked a bit stricken.

"What is it now, Martha?" asked Lucinda impatiently.

"What of Ursula? We could fail to reach her in time to help with Triton. The wedding is tonight right before sunset. She will need our magic to complete the spell once she has Ariel's soul!"

"And so she will! The Morningstar castle is very near Ursula's realm." Martha didn't look relieved by

Lucinda's words. "What? Speak! I'm tired of your sullen looks, the both of you!" Lucinda had lost all patience with her sisters.

"We're tired of choosing our words so carefully. Tired of sounding so... so... *normal!* Surely Circe should love us as we are!"

"Well, she doesn't! We agreed this was the way! The longer we argue this topic, the less time we have to see to Pflanze and the sea witch! Now, please, let's make our preparations."

The sisters stood at the centre of the room before the fireplace. The large onyx ravens seemed to be looking at them, reminding the sisters of the Dark Fairy's warning. That terrible sense of foreboding crept into their hearts once more as they said the words that would take them to Pflanze.

"We call on the winds, the air and the breeze! To Morningstar Castle as quick as you please!"

That spell, no matter how often they performed it, sent a dropping sensation through the odd sisters' stomachs, as if the floor had fallen out from beneath them. Once recovered from the initial feeling of uneasiness, they rushed to the large round kitchen window to see the landscapes that lay between Ipswich and Morningstar's realm. Travelling among the clouds, unseen by those below, never ceased to delight the witches, and to think Ursula fancied their travelling by chicken feet, like that Romanian witch with the lyrical name.

"It's been a long time since we've seen her, Sister! I wonder how she fares?"

"We have far too many witches to keep track of, my dear. Right now it's Ursula's time. Once we settle this matter with Pflanze," Lucinda said.

CHAPTER XVI

TEA WITH POPINJAY

Morningstar Castle was abustle with servants preparing for the winter solstice. Tulip had decided quite at the last moment that they would go on with the festival as usual even with her mother and father away.

Nanny thought it was good to have something to occupy Tulip while she and Pflanze handled the Circe situation, though she was now having second thoughts about her decision to keep Tulip at court rather than insisting she accompany her mother on the visit to her sister's kingdom, especially now that the odd sisters were swooping down, quite literally, at any moment upon Morningstar Castle.

Nanny was looking out the window, hoping to spy the odd sisters, when she remembered she had promised Tulip it would snow for the solstice. With a casual wave of Nanny's hand, light, powdery snowflakes started to fall from the sky. Tulip would have her snow, and she would be occupied with receiving Prince Popinjay for tea that day. That was the real reason Nanny had decided to let Tulip stay. She wanted to give the two a chance to spend some time together. A chance to fall in love.

Prince Popinjay arrived at the castle for afternoon tea looking rather dashing. Fortunately, he seemed to have left his lute at home and had no mind to sing tunes of Tulip's beauty during their tea. Mr. Hudson showed the young man in, directing him past the maids and footmen readying the castle for the winter solstice, to the morning room, where Tulip was waiting for him.

"Prince Popinjay is here to see you, Princess."

"Thank you, Hudson. Can you please have Violet bring the tea?"

"Yes, right away, Princess."

Tulip motioned to the pink satin divan, inviting him to take a seat. "Please." She perched next to him, hardly knowing what to say. She had always been terrible at that sort of thing, making small talk. Small talk always seemed, well, small. Empty little diversions with chatter about the weather, platitudes to pass the time. But that was what ladies were expected to speak of, not of the giants that ruled the lands hundreds of years before, or the wars they fought with Oberon and the Tree Lords of the north. Those, however, were the things that inspired her, truly *fascinated* her, and she wanted to know what inspired him.

Violet fortunately came into the room with the tea, which further delayed Tulip's having to make conversation.

"Thank you, Violet, you can place it there."

Violet set the tea tray on the round table before them with a slight clatter.

"I'm so sorry, Princess!"

Tulip didn't mind if those cups became chipped.

In fact, she'd like to toss them into the sea. It was her least favourite set, because its pink flower pattern reminded her of the Beast prince. She would have to remember to have Violet set out the black and silver set the next day for the solstice.

"Not to worry, Violet, that will be all. I will pour." With slightly trembling hands, Tulip poured some tea for the prince. "How do you take it?" she asked.

"With cream and sugar, please, my lady," croaked Prince Popinjay.

She handed him the cup, set upon the matching saucer, willing her hands not to shake and herself to say something. Anything!

"My mother was sorry she couldn't be here to receive you. She is away visiting her sister Queen Leah."

Prince Popinjay was staring at the contents of his cup, too bashful to meet Tulip's gaze and too afraid to speak, should his voice crack again. It seemed Tulip wasn't alone in her nervousness or distaste for small talk.

"She's suffered much sorrow, my aunt. I'm sure you've heard what's happened to her daughter?"

Popinjay looked up from the exceedingly interesting contents of his teacup and bravely met Tulip's gaze.

"I was very sorry to hear about your cousin." And he continued: "Though I am very pleased you invited me today, Tulip. I was rather surprised when you did."

Tulip's face flushed, making her feel uncomfortable. She wanted to run away.

He's just a prince. Don't be ridiculous, she told herself.

She wanted to be anywhere but there, far away from the prince, with his beautiful haunting grey eyes, in a place where there were no princes at all. Surely there had to be such a place, where there was no reason to make idle small talk about the goings-on in neighbouring kingdoms.

"I was reading about the history of your kingdom and its lands and I found it very fascinating. Did you know there was a great battle fought here?"

With a smile, she asked, "Which one? There were several."

"Oh, I am particularly intrigued by the battle between the Tree Lords and the giants, but they're all so compelling, don't you think?"

And suddenly, Tulip didn't feel the need to flee. In fact, there wasn't a single place in all the kingdoms she'd rather be than with the handsome prince with the haunting grey eyes.

CHAPTER XVII

THE WITCHES' SOLSTICE

Pflanze had been waiting by a castle door for her witches to arrive when in a flash she saw the home she shared with the odd sisters perched on the Morningstar cliffs right above the turbulence of Ursula's watery domain, as if it had always been there.

Perhaps if she hadn't been privy to how her witches' magic worked, she would have thought it *had* always been there; surely that was what the humans would think, and always had thought the many years Pflanze had been travelling with her witches. As much as she had grown to love Nanny and Tulip, she really did miss her witches. She greeted them with her large black-rimmed golden eyes speckled with green. She was sitting almost too perfectly, her white paws primly placed before her while she watched her witches walk the path leading to the castle gate.

"Pflanze, hello!" screamed Martha. "We missed you!" The castle grounds were covered in a light dusting of snow, which was unusual for the coastal kingdom, and the sisters knew a witch was behind it, but who?

The snow clung to the witches' ringlets, looking rather striking in their pitch-black hair. The sisters had almost forgotten it was the winter solstice, with all their fretting over Circe and their dealings with Ursula. Luckily, they had thought to change from their tattered red dresses into their black silks, which were embroidered with many tiny silver stars cascading across their bodices and onto their voluminous skirts, invoking an enchanted evening sky. The three of them walked as one, as they often did, and seemed to be taking in the splendour of the castle, which was truly magnificent and shining like a beacon of beauty and light. The sky, they thought, was particularly breathtaking at twilight; it was their magic hour, when everything looked perfect and they felt anything was possible. It had been many years since the sisters were invited to call upon royalty, not since they had visited their cousin the old king, father to Snow White.

Visits from the odd sisters had become a thing of dread in most royal circles, so the sisters hardly knew how to act, having actually been invited and made to feel welcome by those not of their ilk. Though they wondered... Something was amiss; there *was* someone of their ilk nearby. They thought they had sensed it while approaching the castle grounds, but figured they were just sensing Ursula nearby.

But it wasn't Ursula, was it? It was something else. Someone else.

Someone completely unexpected. The sisters looked frantically about them, searching the sky for crows, wondering where Maleficent was hiding. Had she enchanted their companion to trick them into some sort of trap?

Poor Unfortunate Soul

Pflanze adjusted her paws, and if cats could have done such things, she would have shaken her head at her mistresses. She almost wished she could let this hilarity continue, seeing her witches twitch and shudder about, searching in vain for Maleficent and her crows, but they hadn't time.

It's not the Dark Fairy, my witches. It's her, the One of Legends. Pflanze saw the looks on her witches' faces and knew they understood. *Good,* she thought. *Now let's hope they can put their differences aside long enough to deal with this problem.*

They hadn't time to dwell on past events. It was going to be difficult enough without Nanny and the odd sisters sniping at each other over some long-forgotten dealings, even with the Morningstars out of the way, with the king on business, the queen shipped off to her sister's to calm her nerves, and Tulip entertaining Prince Popinjay for tea.

"So where is she, then?" asked Lucinda, but she saw for herself. Tulip's nanny, with her silver hair and snow-white paper-thin skin, looked impossibly old, older perhaps than she herself knew. She was standing at the threshold with a broad smile and a twinkle in her eye, waiting to welcome them.

"Hello, sisters. Come in. You are most welcome." The sisters and their beautiful cat followed Nanny into the grand vestibule. The entire castle was filled with candlelight, casting an unearthly glow on the ladies that softened their features, reminding the sisters of their younger days. "The castle looks beautiful," said Ruby, admiring the light dancing on the walls.

"Queen Morningstar regrets not greeting you herself. She is currently recovering from recent events abroad with her sister, who, as you know, is in need of consoling herself." The sisters knew of whom she was speaking but didn't say. It was Nanny's way of letting them know she remembered what had transpired between them so many years earlier.

"We're happy you found a nice place for yourself here with Tulip. You were always very good with children and domestic concerns," said Lucinda, wondering how much Nanny remembered.

"It looks like you keep to the old customs

here, I'm happy to see. Not even Snow White's stepmother could make a better spectacle of the solstice," said Lucinda as they made their way into the sitting room.

Nanny smiled.

"Please sit down. We have so much to discuss."

Lucinda didn't like being ordered about but decided Nanny was simply being cordial, so the three sisters sat as one on a beautiful red velvet divan across from Nanny. It was quite the picture, the three of them in their splendid black silks sitting on the red divan. Nanny mused they looked like black hollyhocks on a bed of bloodstained earth. Pflanze listened to the witches' thoughts. As always, she carefully kept her own thoughts to herself. She didn't want the sisters to hear this in fragments or random musings. She didn't want to send them into a panic, rendering them useless to everyone, including themselves.

"Pflanze, why are you here? Why did you send for us?" "Yes, Pflanze, why? Why did you leave when Ursula told us her story?" "We were worried

154

about you! Slinking off like a nasty little creature, making us worry when we have so many other things on our minds!" "It's not like you! Not at all. Please explain yourself!"

Pflanze was silent.

"What's wrong with her? Why won't she speak? Have you done something to our Pflanze?"

The sisters rose from the blood-red divan, ready to pounce on Nanny.

"Sit down! Pflanze is fine! We have something important to show you."

"So, the One of Legends has something to show us? She has much to say? When we already have so many important things to do on this day?"

Ruby's eyes widened with glee. "Oh! We're finally rhyming again? How charmingly delightful!" She was clapping with utter joy. She had been waiting for Lucinda to break the strange means of communication she'd been using since Circe's departure.

Martha jumped up from her seat and started stamping her boots, making a terrible clicking noise. "The sisters are free to rhyme at last! Our mundane ways are a thing of the past!" Ruby gave her sister a disappointed look. "I'm sorry, I'm a bit out of practise!" But Ruby joined her sister anyway, and they sung and stomped their feet in a cacophonous choir of bedlam that echoed throughout the castle. They were having the most fun they'd had since Circe left, and they were enjoying themselves thoroughly until Tulip burst into the room.

"What is going on here, ladies?" The sisters looked at the angelic bunny-faced girl like she was an insect, an alien species, which she was when you thought of it, at least to the sisters. After all, everyone within the room was magical except for Tulip, who, by the look on her face, didn't know what to make of the scene, with these strange, deranged women, whoever they might be, jumping up and down like madwomen. Or better, frenzied marionettes who had taken on lives of their own.

Nanny tried to divert Tulip's attention.

"My dear, have you left Popinjay to his own

devices alone in the morning room?"

"No, Nanny, of course not. He's left," she said rather offhandedly, distracted by these strange sisters who were stomping and singing the castle down.

"Ladies, please. Stop this at once. You're going to step on my cat!" snapped Tulip.

The odd sisters froze, their faces stern and filled with contempt. They resembled baleful dolls, staring at Tulip with their bulging eyes. "*Your* cat?" asked Lucinda, giving Tulip a deadly look.

"Yes, my cat! Now kindly step away from her before you stomp on her with your pointy boots!"

"Lucinda, you will not touch her. She was almost killed by your wicked meddling with the Beast prince. I won't have you hurting my precious girl again!" Tulip had never heard Nanny speak so seriously in all the years she'd known her, not even when she'd confronted Ursula.

"What has she to do with the Beast?" asked Tulip, looking from the sisters to her nanny, confounded. "Who are these women?"

Nanny placed her hand on Tulip's arm to

calm her.

"They are Circe's sisters, dear. They're here to help us find her."

Circe's sisters? Can that be true? Tulip looked at the odd sisters, for surely they were sisters. They had to be; they looked exactly like each other in every respect. There was something sinister about them, something foul. She didn't like the look of them now that she had a chance to take in the entire scene. Their hair was black as a bucket of tar, their skin was white as a cuttlefish bone, and their overly large eyes were lined with black, making them look rather more deep-set than they ought to have been. They were painfully thin, these sisters, with long skeletal hands adorned with rings that hung loose on their bony fingers.

It looked as though a necromancer had summoned them from the grave for the Samhain ball. There was no way the frightful hags were related to Circe.

No way at all.

"Be careful, dear, or we might take the bell in

your soul," said Lucinda, laughing.

"Blight her, Lucinda! She's stolen our cat!"
"We can boil her in oil and give her bones to the Romanian witch as an offering!"

"Calm yourselves, Sisters," said Lucinda, laughing. "She's stolen nothing. Remember, our Pflanze lived in the Beast prince's castle when he was engaged to Tulip. She didn't know she belonged to us. How could she?"

Nanny was surprised that Lucinda was being so sensible. Still, Ruby and Martha were seized by little twitches, trying to contain their anger. They had been so reserved the past several months, so quiet, so unlike themselves. It took all their willpower to keep themselves from opening a door to Hades right there and then and shoving the little brat within so they'd never have to see her stupid angelic face again.

"Watch your thoughts, good sisters," warned Nanny.

"So the One of Legends has remembered she's a telepathist."

Tulip felt she might be losing her mind.

"Who is this One of Legends they speak of?" she asked.

The sisters laughed. Tulip's head spun; she felt like she was caught within their laughter and she would never escape.

"Why, it's your dear sweet nanny. Didn't you know, my dear? She's a witch like... us." Martha cackled.

Tulip backed away from the witches as if they were deadly serpents.

"You're *what?*"

The witches could see Tulip trying to take it all in. Nanny felt she had made a horrible mistake not sending Tulip away while she dealt with this matter. She hadn't wanted to diminish the princess's chances with Popinjay, but this wasn't working. It was a disaster. There was far too much to explain to Tulip to make her understand, and they were losing time.

"I'm sorry, my dear heart, but I think it's time for you to sleep."

Tulip looked dazed, as if in a waking dream. "Yes, if you'll excuse me, I think I will go rest now."

With a kiss for her nanny, Tulip went off to her rooms, where she would stay until Nanny went to wake her.

"I see you remember how to put young girls to sleep," said Lucinda, laughing. It had been a very long time since Lucinda had laughed; she had laughed more on that day than she had in several months and thought it was a very fine thing. Her sisters seemed to agree, because they joined her. Their laughter swelled and fed upon itself, becoming louder and wickeder until it filled the entire sitting room, shaking it and rattling the chandeliers.

No, witches, no!

It was Pflanze, making her thoughts known to all the witches.

You will catch this beautiful room on fire! she said, looking up at the chandelier bouncing about, jostling the lit candles.

"Ladies, tea is waiting for us in the solarium. The view is much better there and the room is less, ah... combustible," said Nanny as the footmen came into the room. She turned to them. "The princess is very vexed from her ordeals over the past several days, so I gave her something to soothe her nerves. Could you please tell Rose to make sure she's made it to her rooms?"

"Yes, mum."

"Now, let's go help ourselves to some tea."

The witches made their way to the solarium down a long hallway with striking murals, which looked particularly lovely in the golden candlelight. Tea was waiting for them, with tiny pink frosted cakes, scones with clotted cream and lemon curd and a beautiful cherry and walnut cake. Ruby sneakily slipped one of the black-and-silver teacups into her purse while fawning over the selection of confections.

"What a lovely tea, Nanny. Very thoughtful."

The main room was astonishingly beautiful, with its glass-domed ceilings and breathtaking view of the rest of the Lighthouse of the Gods. The twilight sky was darkening, and sunset was almost upon them. The witches were growing nervous about the part they must play in Ursula's plot.

"That's why we're here, sisters. We know what

you're planning with Ursula."

Lucinda was quick to anger. "Has the Dark Fairy contacted you, then? Did she send you her odious warning, as well?"

Nanny hadn't heard from the Dark Fairy in ages. In fact, she had forgotten all about her until recently, much like her powers. She had lost her memories before coming to the Morningstar court.

"No, I can't imagine she'd be involved with this madness," she said as Martha scoffed.

"She was always a favourite of yours, wasn't she? Always so perfect. She could never do wrong in your eyes, not even when she destroyed the Fairylands in a fit of rage."

Nanny sighed. "I thought she was *your* friend."

"And so she is," said Lucinda. "But I won't have her interfering with our plans to find Circe! She has crossed the line with us far too many times. It's time she was knocked down from the lofty place she's set herself upon!"

Nanny was growing impatient.

"We're not here to discuss Maleficent! Her story

is too long and complicated to debate in the time we have left, but I am interested in this warning she sent you."

Lucinda rolled her eyes. "It was nothing. I won't discuss it."

Then, giving Nanny a sly look, she continued. "I'd rather discuss how you came to remember who you are. How long were you here among the Morningstars, not knowing your own powers? Not remembering?" She smiled. "I wonder just how much you truly remember."

Nanny remained calm and gracious in the face of Lucinda's torments.

"I am remembering more with every moment, my dear, ever since Pflanze came to court. Though truly I think it began when I was in her company while visiting the Beast prince, though I didn't know it at the time. I suppose I should thank you, sisters, for sending her there to spy."

Martha and Ruby looked at Pflanze, outraged. "Pflanze! How could you betray our secrets?"

Nanny laughed at the sisters.

"Pflanze didn't betray you!"

Ruby and Martha were pacing with worry.

"Lucinda, how could you send our cat to the One of Legends? She's turned her against us!"

Lucinda closed her eyes, willing herself not to strangle her sisters. "How was I supposed to know she was Tulip's nanny? She didn't possess her powers! There was no means to track her! For all I knew, she was dead."

Pflanze was sitting quietly and patiently in front of the enormous solstice tree while the witches argued. The tree towered to the heights of the domed ceiling. She was watching the silver decorations reflect the candlelight and the light casting itself about the room. But her attention was diverted to the debacle of her plans. How could she have thought she could bring these witches together and accomplish anything at all, let alone save Circe's life?

"What do you mean 'save Circe's life'?" asked Lucinda, who was in a frenzy. "What do you mean? Is Circe in danger?" Pflanze breathed in heavily and let her breath out slowly, sighing. She had made a terrible mistake. She had to try to keep her witches from losing their minds; she needed them *sane*. She needed to show them what had happened. Words could be interrupted, twisted and misunderstood.

She needed to *show* her witches; then they would understand. Then they would know.

"Show us what?" The sisters were on their feet again, screaming and clicking their shiny black-pointed boots. "Show us Circe! Show us our sister!" The glass in the domed ceiling was rattling, threatening to shatter, but the sisters didn't seem to take notice or care.

"Show us Circe!"

"Calm yourselves, please! You'll have glass raining down on our heads!" Nanny shouted.

The sisters were in a rampant delirium, screaming and ripping the ribbons in their hair. Their ringlets were in tangles and their makeup was smeared from crying.

"Show us our sister! *Lucinda, use the mirror!*" shouted Martha.

Lucinda snatched Ruby's purse and took out the

enchanted hand mirror.

"Lucinda, we've tried summoning her in the mirror! It doesn't work!" yelled Ruby, but Lucinda wasn't listening.

"Show us Circe!" Lucinda screamed at her terrified reflection in the mirror.

Nanny snatched the mirror from Lucinda's shaking hand. "Show us Circe!"

A strange sickly creature appeared in the mirror. It was a horrid greenish grey with deep blackened pits for eyes.

"Damn this mirror to nothingness! Show us our sister!"

"That is your sister, my dears. That creature *is* Circe."

Poor Unfortunate Soul

Chapter XVIII

The Betrayal of the Sea Witch

The odd sisters sat in disbelief as they looked into their enchanted hand mirror. Their poor dear little sister! How could this creature be their Circe? And why was the One of Legends able to conjure her when they could not?

"I asked Pflanze to bring you here because I'm afraid Ursula is going to break her deal," Nanny said solemnly.

"What deal?" chimed the sisters as one.

"I don't think she plans to give Circe back, like she promised you."

The sisters' heads cocked to the left in a quick jerk. They seemed to be looking at something very far away, in almost a trancelike state, until Lucinda finally responded. "Give her back? What do you mean give her back?"

"I'm sorry, I assumed you knew."

"Knew what? What in Hades are we supposed to know?"

"That Ursula took Circe. I thought that's why you were helping her."

"No, we called her for help. She said she'd help us find Circe once we destroyed Triton."

"I see, so you agreed to ruin Ariel and kill Triton for your own pleasure?"

"Not for pleasure! For Circe! Ursula told us her tale and gathered our hate so we could destroy Triton together! In return she was to help us find our sister! Now our hate will rain down on her like a thousand nightmares for betraying us! She will live in baleful agony beyond the end of her days for this!"

Lucinda rose to her feet. Her sisters remained sitting, utterly astounded that Ursula had used them so shamelessly. Clearly Ursula hadn't been lying about her brother; they had seen the proof of Triton's treachery in the divination fires.

"Triton truly deserves to die, there was no question, so why this betrayal?" Lucinda screamed. "There was no need to deceive us! I don't understand. Perhaps Ursula thought we would refuse her. We would have helped no matter, and what if we *had* refused? Was she going to threaten us with the life of our sister? Blackmail!"

Lucinda was raging with anger, clutching the hand mirror. "Where is Ursula now? Show me the sea witch!"

Vanessa appeared in the mirror. She was on the wedding ship, looking like a maniacal bride. Her pallor was almost ghastly. It was as if her anger was starting to distort her lovely guise and the sea witch was now melding with Vanessa. Ariel was lying on the deck of the ship and Eric was looking on in horror as Vanessa bellowed, "You're too late! You're too late!"

Lightning burst from her fingertips, penetrating the sky like the worst of storms, before her true form exploded from her human shell, causing everyone on the ship to scream in horror, as she crawled along the deck like a slithering thing of nightmares towards Eric and the little mermaid.

"She has Ariel!" screamed Ruby. "We're too late!"

Lucinda clutched the mirror and said, "No. No we're not!"

She cast her hand at the chamber door, sealing it with her magic so none of the servants would be able to get in. She moved to the centre of the room and stood beneath the glass dome. The sky exploded with light as fireworks burst above their heads, raining down upon the dome. Ships had been gathering near Morningstar Castle all evening for the winter solstice, there to pay tribute to the Lighthouse of the Gods with offerings of fire and light. Lucinda recited a new incantation.

"Kill the witch and make her bleed, release our sister, my words you'll heed!"

Ursula's brother appeared in the mirror, his face full of wrath. "Let her go!" he yelled at Ursula, who had Ariel in her grasp. Ursula laughed.

"Not a chance, Triton! She's mine now. We made a deal!"

Ursula showed Triton the contract Ariel had signed, and wondered what was going through his mind. Was he frightened for his daughter's life? *Perhaps I should make him watch while I kill his precious child. Make him suffer the pain and fear my father felt before his death, the death he said my father deserved!*

"Daddy, I'm sorry. I didn't mean to! I didn't know!" cried Ariel.

Triton's anger was growing with each breath, swelling, until he released his rage at Ursula, slamming her into a rock with the power of his trident, trying in vain to break the contract.

"You see! The contract is legal, binding and completely unbreakable, even for you."

Then she smiled at him, in that way she knew he hated, the smile that meant she couldn't wait to see him choke on her hate.

"Of course I was always a girl with an eye for a bargain. The daughter of the great sea king is a very precious commodity."

POOR UNFORTUNATE SOUL

And, I daresay, the little sister of the dreaded three is even more so, she thought.

The odd sisters' anger filled the room like a choking smoke. As much as they hated Triton, they hated Ursula more. *How dare she take our little sister! How dare she use her!*

"Ursula's deceived us, Sisters! She has no intention of letting Circe go!" Ruby's and Martha's screams were heard in the many kingdoms, but Lucinda remained eerily calm.

"Quiet, my darlings, we don't want Ursula to know we've learned her secret. She intends to use our Circe against us, as a tool for bargaining, to ensure our help in her future plans. The Dark Fairy was right. We have to stop her."

The witches again began their chant, which grew louder and more violent as their bodies convulsed and contorted with every word...

"Slice the witch and make her bleed, kill the witch, my words you'll heed!"

...and they watched Ursula and Triton in their magic mirror.

174

"But I might be willing to make an exchange for someone even better," Ursula said.

Triton knew what she wanted. It had never been Ariel; it was *him*. His power. His soul. This was her vengeance and part of him felt he deserved it. He had chased his daughter away with his hatred of humans and brought madness upon his sister with his betrayal of her. *Yes, this is what I deserve,* he thought. He would take his daughter's place. Ursula's words rang in his ears as he signed the contract: *If I am this foul creature you describe, it's by your design!* Ursula had been right when she said that. He had created this monster and there was nothing he could do to amend it. His regret would mean nothing to her. His words would be like ashes.

At least I will be able to save Ariel. Perhaps she will rule with more compassion than I ever had. The sisters watched and wished they could destroy the king as they had intended. It wasn't enough that he finally lamented what he had done to his sister. They wanted him to die. It took all their strength to rein in their hate of Triton and focus it on Ursula, so long had they gathered it, cultivated it and given it life. It took all their might not to succumb to it and kill the tyrant king.

Oh, *how* they wished Ursula was the friend they had thought she was. They would have loved to take down her brother and put her on the throne. They would have done anything to help their friend. Why the betrayal? It was such a disappointment, seeing Ursula fail in the face of such promise. They had thought she was different. She wanted nothing more than revenge and power, because she'd spent her life feeling powerless. She'd become the thing her brother accused her of. She had become loathsome.

Fear gripped the witches' hearts when they saw that Ursula had seized Triton's crown and trident. *This is why the Dark Fairy sent her warning. She knows Ursula's heart better than we do.* And the sisters watched in terror as Ursula grew to prodigious heights.

The madness within her also seemed to grow with an unnerving velocity. Her laugh dominated the many kingdoms as she commanded the sea, bringing forth ships that had long before sunk to the depths. She brought the dead ships to life with the treacherous waves, raving maniacally and claiming the sea as her own.

If there was anything left of the witch the sisters had called "friend", they couldn't detect it. Ursula was completely at the mercy of this overwhelming power, and it had driven her quite mad.

The Dark Fairy was right.

Ursula created a maelstrom of twisting splintered ships and used them to attack Ariel and Eric. She was going to kill Ariel. It seemed her plans to be Eric's bride had been tossed aside like an unwanted plaything, forgotten now with the madness that was swelling inside her.

She's grown mad with power. Perhaps mad with grief, with the loss of everything she once loved.

Lucinda said the words again, this time resolving to destroy the thing she and her sisters had helped create with their hatred. They were no better than Triton, Lucinda thought, because they had played a part in Ursula's undoing, as well. It broke Lucinda's heart and brought her no joy, in spite of the betrayal.

"Kill the witch and make her bleed, release our sister, my words you'll heed!"

Martha and Ruby were in a panic.

"We can't kill Ursula! There has to be a way to save her!" screamed Ruby. "If we take the crown and trident, she'll come back to herself."

"Yes, this is our fault! Circe was right to be angry with us! We're always meddling, and our meddling caused this. It will cost Ursula her life!"

Lucinda cast a terrifying gaze at her sisters. "Silence! This is Ursula's doing, not ours! She would have got her hands on the necklace regardless, and she took our sister as insurance so that we would help her! She is not the witch we once knew. She's been overwhelmed by power and greed just like the Wicked Queen, and we shall destroy her for her duplicity!"

The fireworks burst forth from the ships in Morningstar Harbour and exploded overhead, raining on the dome above the witches as Lucinda went on. "This is the only way to free our sister and ensure she will not hate us until the end of her days! Circe would never forgive us for unleashing this power."

Lucinda looked to the sky through the glass dome, at the storm of sparks cascading down, as the sea raged with a violent purple light. "We have no choice, my sisters. We have to destroy her. Now, say the words with me."

Lucinda, Ruby, Martha and the One of Legends gathered their power and sent it out to the many kingdoms so witches far and wide would hear their call. This was not a secret, dark sort of magic. It was a desperate gathering of forces to take down the witch who now had the power to destroy them all.

"You took our sister and our hate, to die at our hands is now your fate!"

The witches screeched, and taking the mirror once again, they said, "Now show us the witch!" Ursula's image appeared in the enchanted mirror.

"She's trying to kill Ariel! She's broken her deal! Kill the witch now, make her suffering real!"

All the witches were in a frenzy, stomping

their boots and screaming so loudly the glass dome was again threatening to break. The servants were pounding on the door, trying to get in to see what was the matter, frightened of the loud screams coming from inside the room and the terrible explosions coming from the sea.

"Show us the witch!"

The witches watched as Prince Eric climbed onto one of the resurrected ships. Its bow was splintered and jagged, and the witches knew Ursula's death was almost upon them.

"Impale the witch and make her bleed, give Eric the power, our words you'll heed!"

And to their relief, Ursula was violently impaled by the ship's splintered bow in an explosion of electricity and billowing purple smoke, casting her remains deep into the sea.

The sisters collapsed as they watched the voluminous smoke rising from the sea, knowing they had killed the witch they had once called their friend.

CHAPTER XIX

CIRCE'S DESPAIR

Deep within the ocean, tucked away in Ursula's garden of lost souls, Circe felt herself become shining and brilliant, like the dazzling golden lights that surrounded her. It was a curious sensation, as if she had never known what it was to feel alive until that moment. Ursula had taken her soul and left her empty shell to wither with the other victims in the sea witch's garden.

Circe had never contemplated what that would be like, to lose her soul, and she couldn't have imagined what a deep, penetrating sense of emptiness it would bring, as if nothing but sadness and loneliness remained.

But even that didn't adequately describe how it had felt.

She supposed it was similar to powerful grief, that wretched emptiness and feeling of despair and helplessness, as if being swallowed by a deep blackened pit that you were unable to crawl out of.

She wondered if that was how the Beast had felt when the curse took away his humanity, and heat rose to her cheeks as shame washed over her. Of course her sisters would say that he had brought it on himself. That she had given him a choice. And that was true. But it hurt her heart to think she had ever managed to cause such pain to another, even if he had deserved it.

As she and the other victims rose out of Ursula's garden, freed, she saw the ghastly remains of her captor scattered on the ocean floor and knew her sisters were probably nearby. She swam with a mermaid's tail and cringed when she saw large portions of Ursula's severed tentacles, feeling an intense guilt for the part she'd had to play in Ursula's death.

She didn't understand why Ursula had betrayed her, and though she was no longer trapped within Ursula's garden of lost souls, the empty, terrible feeling lingered within her. She just wanted to know why. She had always liked Ursula. She had always been her friend. She would never know why Ursula had betrayed her...

Or would she?

There, glistening on the besmirched and murky ocean floor, lying among Ursula's remains, was the golden seashell necklace. Circe snatched it in her little hand and made a desperate wish.

She was instantly assaulted by a rage she'd never before experienced. The weight of it was impossible to contain; she felt as if it would consume her. No, that wasn't right; it felt like something was growing inside her, something too large and too vile for her to contain. She felt as if she would burst and nothing but hate would remain.

It was unbearable, this pain. This anguish. But the hate and the rage, that was the worst of it. It was like a terrible sickness that wrapped itself around her heart, distorting her mind and filling it with horrific images. Circe's head was filled with visions she didn't understand. Terrible, frightful scenes of a man being slaughtered, pulled literally to pieces by an angry mob, trying to keep it away from a young girl. And images of the same young girl standing on a cliff, crying, her heart full of fear and loathing. The pictures kept flashing one to the other in rapid succession. Circe didn't know what they meant, but she could feel the memories as if they were her own, because she felt herself to be something entirely new, entirely different… alien.

In that moment, she had come to possess the psyche of the sea witch.

She *was* Ursula.

She was leviathan, her body swelling not only with rage but with strength and girth. She had the power to command the sea and she did so at her pleasure. That power was too much for any witch to bear, even Ursula, and it frightened Circe. She fought not only against herself but against an enormous hate being directed at her. She couldn't comprehend who had the power to direct such hatred. Who had the power to use her own magic against her? Her mind whirled at the maelstrom of hate that flooded her. She had grown to immeasurable proportions and felt she was impenetrable. Her hate had betrayed her.

Circe saw into the sea witch's heart. She was foul. She was ugly. She was monstrous and loathsome. She was everything her brother said of her, and everything the Dark Fairy foresaw. And the sea witch had known she deserved that end. She had known it the moment before she died. She had betrayed the odd sisters, her dear friends for this... for this power and for revenge. A power that was destroying her. A power she couldn't control. She had no will of her own. The seething hate had taken possession of her. It was its own creature, and she had no will to command it.

She had been dead before Eric took her life.

Circe pealed a frightful scream so loud and so terrible she thought the force of it would rip her throat.

She was herself again, but diminished, not only from her ordeal but from seeing into Ursula's heart in the sea witch's final moments.

When she reached the surface, she could see purple and black billowing smoke rising from the ocean like a menacing cloud of ruin, filling the sky and blackening the ships that had been docked near Morningstar Castle. Ursula's remains had floated to the surface and mingled with the sea foam, turning it a putrid greyish black. Her hate seemed to linger even after her death.

The Lighthouse of the Gods stood shining in exquisite brilliance, however, as if refusing to be diminished by the foul smoke of decay. As Circe stepped out of the waves and onto land, it was comforting to have feet again and to feel the sand beneath them. She felt her sisters were near, and rushed to the castle in a panic, because she knew there was something horribly wrong.

She didn't bother with the guardsmen at the gate and simply willed them to let her in. Mr. Hudson greeted her at the door with a panic-stricken look. He was pale and his eyes were full of terror.

"Miss Circe, thank the gods you're here! There is something terribly wrong with Princess Tulip, and Nanny has been attacked!" Circe tried to clear her head, which was still muddled from her transformation from mermaid to witch.

"Where are they? Take me to them."

Mr. Hudson directed her to the main room, where several guardsmen were trying to chop their way in with axes, succeeding only in breaking their weapons, which lay in a heap on the floor.

"Stand back, gentlemen." Circe cast her hand forwards, blasting the door inwards with a violent splintering crash.

Nanny and Circe's sisters were lying on the floor, unconscious.

"Where's Tulip?" she asked, looking around the room.

"In her room, miss. Rose has been trying to wake her for hours."

Circe couldn't fathom what had happened.

"I need everyone out of this room."

Mr Hudson tried to protest, but Circe silenced him with an uncustomary sternness.

"Hudson, now! Order everyone out of this room so I can tend to Nanny and my sisters."

CHAPTER XX

TRITON'S REGRET

As Triton made his way through the murky waters, trying to find his daughter, he was sickened by the horrors that surrounded him. He could feel his sister's hate embedded in the decay that littered the ocean floor. He thought he would choke on it and assumed that was her intention. He knew he deserved her hatred, and he felt an overwhelming sense of dread for the part he had played in her demise. There was nothing Triton could do to atone for his malversation towards his sister, but he could make things right with his daughter, even if it meant turning her into a human.

And he thought that Ursula had her vengeance

after all, because he was about to turn someone he loved deeply into the thing he most hated.

A human.

CHAPTER XXI

THE WITCHES' SLEEP

Circe was sitting near Tulip's bed, watching her as she slept. She checked to be sure Tulip wasn't wearing anything unusual that could have cast the sleeping spell, and came to the conclusion that one of the many witches under that roof must have cast the spell, and Circe was unable to break it. She wished she knew what had happened while she was held captive by Ursula. But much of it remained a mystery while Nanny and the sisters were still unconscious. Circe was sitting there holding Tulip's hand, feeling helpless and alone, when she saw a magnificent rainbow soar through the sky over a beautiful ship. The scene sent a surge of joy through her heart, but she didn't know why.

"It's a wedding ship, dear, that's why."

Circe looked up and saw Nanny and Pflanze standing in the doorway.

"Nanny! What's happened?"

Nanny sighed in relief that Circe was safe and their sacrifice hadn't been in vain.

"What sacrifice? Not Tulip?"

Nanny smiled weakly. "No, dear. Tulip will be fine. I can wake her whenever I wish."

And then Circe knew. There was something terribly wrong with her sisters. "Yes, my dear. To reverse magic so embedded with hate took great strength. I'm astonished your sisters survived the ordeal."

Circe now understood why Ursula had felt her own magic was being levelled against her.

"I don't understand. What magic needed reversing? Why would my sisters…" And then she understood. They had done it to release her from Ursula's garden.

"Come, my darling, we should see the wedding ship off, and then we shall have some tea and Nanny will tell you everything."

Nanny could hear Circe's thoughts, her confusion and the myriad questions weighing upon her.

"After you've heard my story, you will be glad you saw the happy couple off to live their life together. Trust me, my dear. Nanny knows your heart almost as well as you do."

POOR UNFORTUNATE SOUL

Epilogue

Two witches, divergent in age and in schools of magic, though with very similar hearts and sensibilities, stood on the windy cliffs as they watched Ariel and Eric's wedding ship sail off into the future. Ariel was happier than she had ever been. She was venturing into an entirely new world with the man she loved. She would finally dance, and run, and know what it was to live and love as she had always imagined.

"My sisters stopped Ursula from killing this girl?"

Nanny decided the simplest answer was best.

"Yes, my dear, they did. Your sisters saved us all."

Circe thought Nanny was right: perhaps in the retelling of the tale she would find pleasure in the little mermaid's story, and she would be happy that Ariel's wish to become human and marry her prince came true. But for now she could only think of her sisters and of Pflanze sitting beside them, watching silently with fearful eyes, waiting and wishing for her mistresses to wake from their deathlike sleep.

Then a shiver came over Nanny and Circe, a tingling sensation at the backs of their necks that told them someone was coming.

A witch.

A powerful witch. But neither could make out her intentions.

THE END

A Twisted Tale

Unravel new twists in the tales that you already know and love in this series of thrilling novels.

As Old As Time

What if Belle's mother cursed the beast?

Belle makes an intriguing discovery about her own mother as she starts to unravel the secrets about the Beast's curse.

A Whole New World

What if Aladdin had never found the lamp?

Evil Jafar has possession of the magical lamp and the power-mad ruler is determined to take control of life and death.

Once Upon a Dream

What if the sleeping beauty never woke up?

As the prince prepares to kiss the sleeping princess, he too falls into a deep sleep and the fairytale is far from over.

Reflection

What if Mulan had to travel to the Underworld?

Still disguised as the soldier Ping, Mulan faces a deadly battle in a mysterious world as she tries to save the life of Captain Shang.